U0084398

序 言

　　根據「九年一貫教育」的課程標準，國中生要有 2000 個單字的程度，過去只要背 800 多個，現在突然增加為 2000 個，所以同學應該朝這個方向去努力，單字背愈多愈好。

　　我們將這 2000 個單字中，太簡單的字彙，或不適合做字彙題的單字刪除，再加上 2000 字之外，在基本學力測驗中常考的字彙，約 500 個字左右，這 500 個單字，也就是升高中的關鍵字彙。考來考去就這 500 個，同學讀完這本單字手冊，在字彙一項，就可以得到滿分。

　　字彙也是閱讀與寫作的基礎，本書收錄考試出現頻率特別高的字彙，編成典型考題，供同學練習。若干單字並附解析，幫助同學記憶。每隔八頁又附有 Check List，供同學自我評量之用。

　　本書雖精心編排並仔細校對，但仍恐有疏漏，竭誠歡迎讀者指正或賜教。

劉 毅

【本書製作過程】

本書集結無數模擬試題，挑選出常考的單字，再將出現頻率高的單字，做成典型考題。全書由張碧紋老師擔任總指揮，感謝周宛靜小姐及張家慈小姐協助整理資料，白雪嬌小姐設計封面，黃淑貞小姐負責打字，王淑平小姐校對音標並貼插圖，謝靜芳老師及 Laura E. Stewart 老師擔任總校訂，大家一起努力，把這本書完成，我以堅強的編輯團隊為榮，我對他們的努力深表感謝。

名 詞

accident 〔'æksədənt 〕 *n.* 意外

Last winter there were a lot of car *accidents* because of the ice on the roads.

【典型考題】

I saw a terrible ＿＿＿＿＿ on my way to school yesterday.

(A) story   (B) experience
(C) news   (D) accident

答案：**D**

actor 〔'æktə 〕 *n.* 演員

Tom Cruise is really a good *actor*.

actress 〔'æktrɪs 〕 *n.* 女演員

Halle Berry won the Best *Actress* award in this year's Oscars.

* award 〔ə'wɔrd 〕 *n.* 獎　　***Oscars*** 奧斯卡獎

address (ə'drɛs) *n.* 地址

<u>dress</u> 洋裝
<u>add</u>ress 地址

Jack wrote the *address*

on the envelope and mailed the letter.

age (edʒ) *n.* 年紀

Children in Taiwan enter elementary

school at the *age* of seven or eight.

appointment (ə'pɔɪntmənt) *n.* 約會

I have made an *appointment* with my

family doctor for three o'clock.

appoint	+	ment
指定	+	*n.*

【典型考題】

She made a(n) _____ with the

dentist for three this afternoon.

(A) appointment　　(B) address

(C) airplane　　(D) afternoon

答案：**A**

April (ˋeprəl) *n.* 四月

Why don't we play a trick on our teacher on *April* Fool's Day?

art (ɑrt) *n.* 藝術

Monica is interested in many kinds of *art*, especially painting.

artist (ˋɑrtɪst) *n.* 藝術家

Van Gogh was a famous *artist*.

art ＋ ist
｜　　｜
藝術 ＋ 人

beach (bitʃ) *n.* 海灘

Formosa is an island famous for its friendly people and beautiful *beaches*.

【典型考題】

We are going to the _____ on Sunday.

(A) ball   (B) cook

(C) beach   (D) spring

答案：**C**

bedtime ('bɛd,taɪm) *n.* 就寢時間

When I was a little child, my parents always told me *bedtime* stories.

> time 時間
> bed<u>time</u> 就寢時間

beef (bif) *n.* 牛肉

Which do you like, *beef* or pork?

bicycle ('baɪsɪkḷ) *n.* 腳踏車

You'll never learn to ride a *bicycle* if you don't practice.

【典型考題】

A: Can you ride a _____?
B: Yes, I can.

(A) bakery   (B) bread
(C) barber   (D) bicycle

答案：**D**

bill〔bɪl〕*n.* 帳單

I forgot to pay my cell phone *bill* last month, so I can't call out now.

* *cell phone* 手機

【典型考題】

The _____ is so large that I am afraid I can't pay it.

(A) bell　　　　　　(B) bill
(C) bus　　　　　　(D) bite

答案：**B**

billion〔'bɪljən〕*n.* 十億

I bet you a *billion* dollars that Monica will marry me.

| bill 帳單 |
| billion 十億 |

breakfast〔'brɛkfəst〕*n.* 早餐

At what time do you have *breakfast* every morning?

bush 〔 buʃ 〕 *n.* 灌木叢

Say what you mean — don't beat about the *bush*.

* ***beat about the bush*** 拐彎抹角

businessman 〔ˈbɪznɪsˌmæn 〕 *n.* 商人

Mr. Wang is a successful *businessman* who owns a big factory.

business	+	man
商業	+	人

【典型考題】

A good _____ usually does business well and contributes to his country.

(A) businessman   (B) reporter

(C) dancer   (D) musician

答案：**A**

cake 〔 kek 〕 *n.* 蛋糕

Lucy said the math test was difficult, but I thought it was a piece of *cake*.

* ***a piece of cake*** 很容易

calculator (ˋkælkjə͵letɚ) *n.* 計算機

It'll be easier to work out this math
problem if you use
a *calculator*.

calculat + or
| 　　 |
計算 + 物

cancer (ˋkænsɚ) *n.* 癌症

<u>can</u> 能夠
<u>can</u>cer 癌症

Some people may get
cancer from secondhand smoke.

* *secondhand smoke* 二手煙

【典型考題】

It is a pity that the beautiful girl got _____.
(A) flower　　　　　(B) cancer
(C) hope　　　　　　(D) wish

答案：**B**

care (kɛr) *n.* 照顧

The nurse can take good *care* of the
sick man.

cash 〔kæʃ〕 *n.* 現金

We don't accept credit cards, so you can only pay in *cash*.

ceiling 〔'silɪŋ〕 *n.* 天花板

My brother is tall enough to touch the *ceiling* of my house.

celebration 〔ˌsɛlə'breʃən〕 *n.* 慶祝

A party will be held in *celebration* of the school's 100th birthday.

celebrat + ion
|　　　|
慶祝　 + *n.*

【典型考題】

We held a party in _____ of our wedding anniversary.

(A) decoration　　　(B) concentration
(C) decision　　　　(D) celebration

答案：**D**

- ☐ artist _____
- ☐ bedtime _____
- ☐ ceiling _____
- ☐ cancer _____
- ☐ actor _____

- ☐ beach _____
- ☐ art _____
- ☐ actress _____
- ☐ billion _____
- ☐ cake _____

- ☐ care _____
- ☐ calculator _____
- ☐ celebration _____
- ☐ April _____
- ☐ accident _____

Check List

1. 十　億　　b _____billion_____ n
2. 商　人　　b _____ n
3. 癌　症　　c _____ r
4. 意　外　　a _____ t
5. 牛　肉　　b _____ f

6. 約　會　　a _____ t
7. 藝術家　　a _____ t
8. 現　金　　c _____ h
9. 海　灘　　b _____ h
10. 計算機　　c _____ r

11. 早　餐　　b _____ t
12. 帳　單　　b _____ l
13. 地　址　　a _____ s
14. 年　紀　　a _____ e
15. 慶　祝　　c _____ n

chance 〔 tʃæns 〕 *n.* 機會

I met an old friend by *chance* while I was walking down the street.

* ***by chance*** 偶然地   down 〔 daʊn 〕 *prep.* 沿著

【典型考題】

It's the _____ of a lifetime. Don't miss it , or you'll regret (後悔) it.

(A) change   (B) chicken

(C) chance   (D) charge

答案：**C**

change 〔 tʃendʒ 〕 *n.* 改變

Instead of eating at home again, why don't we go to a restaurant for a *change*?

【典型考題】

Did you notice the _____ in his expression (表情) ? He is a suspect (嫌疑犯).

(A) change   (B) leg

(C) garden   (D) jacket

答案：**A**

channel 〔ˈtʃænḷ〕 *n.* 管道；頻道

Before long, the new government will open a *channel* of communication with Japan.

* government 〔ˈgʌvənmənt〕 *n.* 政府

check 〔tʃɛk〕 *n.* 支票

Please write me a *check* for ten thousand dollars.

children 〔ˈtʃɪldrən〕 *n. pl.* 孩子

How many *children* do you have?

【典型考題】

_____ can go on a study tour during summer vacation.

(A) Churches   (B) Christmas

(C) Roads   (D) Children

答案：**D**

chocolate (ˈtʃɔkəlɪt) *n.* 巧克力

The *chocolate* cake looks so delicious.
I can't wait to eat it.

【典型考題】

Don't eat too much _____, or you'll
gain weight easily.

(A) vegetable   (B) air conditioner

(C) chocolate   (D) dishes

答案：**C**

church (tʃɝtʃ) *n.* 教堂

When people feel worried about
something, they often go to *church*
to pray.

* pray (pre) *v.* 祈禱

closet (ˈklɑzɪt) *n.* 衣櫥

Put the jackets and coats in the *closet* if
you don't need them.

coffee 〔'kɔfɪ 〕 *n.* 咖啡

My father owns a *coffee* shop around the corner.

communication 〔 kə,mjunə'keʃən 〕 *n.* 通訊

After the typhoon, all *communication* was broken off.

* ***break off*** 切斷

communicat + ion 溝通
溝通   +   *n.*

【典型考題】

E-mail is a very convenient form of

_____.

(A) exercise   (B) experience
(C) vacation   (D) communication

答案：**D**

computer 〔 kəm'pjutɚ 〕 *n.* 電腦

We can send e-mail on the *computer*.

【典型考題】

I like to use a(n) _____ when I type
my reports.

(A) telephone　　　(B) computer

(C) umbrella　　　(D) calculator

答案：**B**

convenience 〔 kən'vinjəns 〕 *n.* 方便

People may go to a *convenience* store
to buy ice cream or soft drinks.

＊ *soft drink* 不含酒精的飲料
　convenience store 便利商店

【典型考題】

I bought a newspaper at the _____
store.

(A) department　　　(B) clothes

(C) convenience　　　(D) quick

答案：**C**

conversation 〔͵kɑnvɚˈseʃən〕 *n.* 對話

Lily and David were talking in low
voices, so I couldn't hear their
conversation.

cookie 〔ˈkʊkɪ〕 *n.* 餅乾

Cookies are my sister's favorite food.

corner 〔ˈkɔrnɚ〕 *n.* 角落;轉角

Wayne is sitting alone in a *corner* of
the café, lost in thought.

【典型考題】

The bookstore is on the street _____.

(A) park   (B) school

(C) corner   (D) parking lot

答案:**C**

country 〔ˈkʌntrɪ〕 *n.* 國家

There are many developing *countries* in Asia.

* developing 〔dɪˈvɛləpɪŋ〕*adj.* 開發中的

【典型考題】

This _____ has been at war (戰爭) for several years.

(A) country   (B) restaurant
(C) ocean   (D) singer

答案：**A**

credit 〔ˈkrɛdɪt〕*n.* 信用

Kelly used her *credit* card to buy a washing machine.

decision 〔dɪˈsɪʒən〕*n.* 決定

Susan is a mature girl who can make her own *decisions*.

* mature 〔məˈtʃʊr〕*adj.* 成熟的

decoration 〔ˌdɛkəˈreʃən〕 *n.* 裝飾品

People usually put a lot of *decorations* on the Christmas tree.

decorat + ion
裝飾 + *n.*

【典型考題】

The ＿＿＿＿＿ in the department store attract customers.

(A) checks   (B) decorations

(C) high prices   (D) cars

答案：**B**

dentist 〔ˈdɛntɪst〕 *n.* 牙醫

"Oh, my tooth hurts!" "That's too bad. You should go to the *dentist*."

* tooth 〔tuθ〕 *n.* 牙齒

☐ coffee　　　　＿＿＿＿＿＿＿

☐ country　　　　＿＿＿＿＿＿＿

☐ dentist　　　　＿＿＿＿＿＿＿

☐ change　　　　＿＿＿＿＿＿＿

☐ chance　　　　＿＿＿＿＿＿＿

☐ cookie　　　　＿＿＿＿＿＿＿

☐ decoration　　　＿＿＿＿＿＿＿

☐ computer　　　＿＿＿＿＿＿＿

☐ decision　　　　＿＿＿＿＿＿＿

☐ channel　　　　＿＿＿＿＿＿＿

☐ corner　　　　＿＿＿＿＿＿＿

☐ convenience　　＿＿＿＿＿＿＿

☐ children　　　　＿＿＿＿＿＿＿

☐ closet　　　　　＿＿＿＿＿＿＿

☐ chocolate　　　＿＿＿＿＿＿＿

Check List

1.	改　變	c _____*change*_____ e
2.	管　道	c _____ l
3.	裝飾品	d _____ n
4.	孩　子	c _____ n
5.	教　堂	c _____ h
6.	衣　櫥	c _____ t
7.	信　用	c _____ t
8.	電　腦	c _____ r
9.	國　家	c _____ y
10.	對　話	c _____ n
11.	方　便	c _____ e
12.	巧克力	c _____ e
13.	轉　角	c _____ r
14.	決　定	d _____ n
15.	牙　醫	d _____ t

dessert ﹝ dɪˈzɝt ﹞ *n.* 甜點

Which would you like for *dessert*, ice cream or fresh fruit?

dialogue ﹝ˈdaɪəˌlɔg ﹞ *n.* 對話

A *dialogue* between the East and the West is necessary.

【典型考題】

I don't want to talk to you anymore. This really is a meaningless _____.

(A) fun   (B) dialogue

(C) chance   (D) desert

答案：**B**

dictionary 〔'dɪkʃən,ɛrɪ 〕 *n.* 字典

He looked up the new word in the *dictionary*.

* *look up* 查閱

【典型考題】

I didn't know what the word meant, so I looked it up in the _____.

(A) calculator   (B) dictionary

(C) telephone   (D) album

答案:**B**

diet 〔'daɪət 〕 *n.* 飲食

I'm too heavy. I should go on a *diet*.

* *go on a diet* 節食

【典型考題】

Tim lost ten kilos by going on a _____.

(A) vacation   (B) hospital

(C) diet   (D) bus

答案:**C**

difference ('dɪfərəns) *n.* 不同；差異

It is hard for me to tell the *difference* between the twins.

differ	+	ence
不同	+	*n.*

* tell (tɛl) *v.* 看出
  twins (twɪnz) *n. pl.* 雙胞胎

【典型考題】

Even though they are twins, there are still a lot of _____ between them.

(A) looks   (B) likes

(C) differences   (D) coats

答案：**C**

dining room ('daɪnɪŋ‚rum) *n.* 飯廳

Every Sunday evening, we have dinner together in the *dining room*.

doll 〔dɑl〕 *n.* 洋娃娃

Everyone says Victoria's daughter is just like a pretty *doll*.

* pretty 〔'prɪtɪ〕 *adj.* 漂亮的

【典型考題】

The little girl wants a ＿＿＿＿＿ for her birthday.
(A) doll   (B) diet
(C) test   (D) music

答案：**A**

dollar 〔'dɑlɚ〕 *n.* 元

The dictionary cost me seven hundred *dollars*.

driver 〔'draɪvɚ〕 *n.* 駕駛人

The drunk *driver* died in the accident yesterday.

* drunk 〔drʌŋk〕 *adj.* 喝醉的

earthquake〔'ɝθ͵kwek〕*n.* 地震

I'm worried about my family because I haven't been able to contact them since the *earthquake*.

* contact〔'kɑntækt〕*v.* 連絡

【典型考題】

The ＿＿＿＿＿ made the building fall down.

(A) earth
(B) earthquake
(C) ball
(D) umbrella

答案：**B**

electricity〔ɪ͵lɛk'trɪsətɪ〕*n.* 電

When a typhoon comes, the *electricity* might go off. We should get a flashlight.

* **go off** （電）停止供應
flashlight〔'flæʃ͵laɪt〕*n.* 手電筒

elephant 〔'ɛləfənt 〕 *n.* 大象

The *elephant* is the biggest animal on land.

e-mail 〔'i,mel 〕 *n.* 電子郵件

For many people, sending and getting
e-mail has become a part of their lives.

【典型考題】

I sent a(n) ＿＿＿＿＿ to my friend in China.
(A) mother   (B) e-mail
(C) telephone call   (D) experience

答案：**B**

emotion 〔 ɪ'moʃən 〕 *n.* 情感

He is a man of strong *emotion*.

end 〔 ɛnd 〕 *n.* 末尾；結束

We are going on a graduation trip at the
end of this semester.

* *graduation trip* 畢業旅行
   semester 〔 sə'mɛstə 〕 *n.* 學期

envelope〔'ɛnvə,lop〕*n.* 信封

Children are very happy to get red *envelopes* from relatives on Chinese New Year.

* **red envelope** 紅包

  relative〔'rɛlətɪv〕*n.* 親戚

【典型考題】

Remember to put a stamp on the ＿＿＿＿＿ before you mail the letter.

(A) e-mail   (B) envelope

(C) post office   (D) corner

答案：**B**

exam〔ɪg'zæm〕*n.* 考試

The *exam* today was the most difficult one we've ever had to take.

* **take an exam** 參加考試

example 〔 ɪgˋzæmpḷ 〕 *n.* 榜樣；例子

Please follow your brother's *example* and be a good boy.

* *follow one's example* 以某人爲榜樣

【典型考題】

The teacher gave me a(n) _____ to help me understand.

(A) excuse   (B) temperature
(C) example   (D) telephone

答案：**C**

excuse 〔 ɪkˋskjus 〕 *n.* 藉口

Diana made up a very good *excuse* for why she was late for class.

* *make up* 編造

exercise 〔ˋɛksə͵saɪz 〕 *n.* 運動

You are too weak. You need to take more *exercise* every day.

- [ ] excuse   _____
- [ ] dictionary   _____
- [ ] diet   _____
- [ ] doll   _____
- [ ] exercise   _____

- [ ] electricity   _____
- [ ] dialogue   _____
- [ ] emotion   _____
- [ ] earthquake   _____
- [ ] dessert   _____

- [ ] difference   _____
- [ ] example   _____
- [ ] envelope   _____
- [ ] dollar   _____
- [ ] driver   _____

1. 對　話　d ___dialogue___ e
2. 字　典　d _____ y
3. 電　　　e _____ y
4. 榜　樣　e _____ e
5. 運　動　e _____ e

6. 飲　食　d _____ t
7. 洋娃娃　d _____ l
8. 大　象　e _____ t
9. 不　同　d _____ e
10. 藉　口　e _____ e

11. 情　感　e _____ n
12. 信　封　e _____ e
13. 元　　　d _____ r
14. 駕駛人　d _____ r
15. 地　震　e _____ e

experience ﹝ ɪkˈspɪrɪəns ﹞ *n.* 經驗

Karen has ten years of *experience* in teaching.

【典型考題】

The doctor has a lot of _____ with cancer patients, so I think he is a good doctor.

(A) accidents   (B) experience
(C) expert   (D) lessons

答案：**B**

factory ﹝ˈfæktrɪ﹞ *n.* 工廠

Mr. Wilson works in a *factory* that produces mainly car parts.

fake ﹝ fek ﹞ *n.* 仿冒品

A famous brand of cell phone can't be that cheap. It must be a *fake*.

* brand ﹝ brænd ﹞ *n.* 品牌

fan 〔 fæn 〕 *n.* (電影、音樂、運動等的) 迷

Linda is a big *fan* of Tom Cruise. She has
seen every movie he has starred in.

* star 〔 stɑr 〕 *v.* 主演

fault 〔 fɔlt 〕 *n.* 過錯

I'm sorry for breaking your window.
It's all my *fault*.

finger 〔 'fɪŋgɚ 〕 *n.* 手指

Good luck in the speech contest. I'll keep
my *fingers* crossed for you.

* *speech contest* 演講比賽
  keep one's fingers crossed 祈求好運

firefighter 〔 'faɪr͵faɪtɚ 〕 *n.* 消防隊員

The *firefighter* saved a woman from a
building that was on fire.

* *on fire* 著火

flashlight ('flæʃ,laɪt) *n.* 手電筒

When there is no electricity, you need a
flashlight in order to see.

* *in order to V.* 為了要~

flight (flaɪt) *n.* 班機

Hurry up! You don't have time to waste.
Your *flight* to Paris is at 2:30.

【典型考題】

Could you tell me what time _____ 212
arrives in New York City?

(A) flight   (B) fruit
(C) wind   (D) air

答案:**A**

floor (flor) *n.* 樓層

This elevator stops at every *floor*.

* elevator ('ɛlə,vetɚ) *n.* 電梯

future 〔'fjutʃɚ〕 *n.* 未來

I want to be an English teacher in the *future*.

garbage 〔'garbɪdʒ〕 *n.* 垃圾

We have to take out the *garbage* after we eat.

garden 〔'gardn̩〕 *n.* 花園

We have only a small *garden*, in which there are a lot of small flowers.

grade 〔 gred 〕 *n.* 分數；成績

We are so surprised that John always gets very good *grades* in math.

【典型考題】

His math ＿＿＿＿＿ was the highest in the class.

(A) homework　　(B) grade
(C) lesson　　(D) teacher

答案：**B**

grandparents 〔'grænd͵pɛrənts 〕 *n. pl.*
祖父母

We live with our *grandparents*.

ground 〔 graʊnd 〕 *n.* 地面

We sat on the *ground* to have lunch.

guitar 〔 gɪ'tɑr 〕 *n.* 吉他

The sound of an electric *guitar* is different
from that of a traditional one.

* ***electric guitar*** 電吉他
    traditional 〔 trə'dɪʃənḷ 〕 *adj.* 傳統的

gym 〔 dʒɪm 〕 *n.* 體育館

We usually play basketball in the school
gym.

happiness ﹝'hæpɪnɪs﹞ *n.* 快樂

His heart was filled with *happiness* when he heard the good news.

harm ﹝hɑrm﹞ *n.* 傷害

Everyone knows that smoking does a lot of *harm* to our health.

history ﹝'hɪstrɪ﹞ *n.* 歷史

The landing of Apollo 11 on the moon made *history*.

* landing ﹝'lændɪŋ﹞ *n.* 登陸

hospital ﹝'hɑspɪtl̩﹞ *n.* 醫院

When you get hurt, you should go to the *hospital*.

【典型考題】

The injured man was taken to the ＿＿＿＿＿＿.

(A) museum   (B) theater

(C) park   (D) hospital

答案：**D**

idea 〔 aɪˈdiə 〕 *n.* 想法

She had to give up the *idea* of visiting the place.

interest 〔ˈɪntrɪst 〕 *n.* 興趣

Do you have any *interest* in collecting stamps?

invention 〔 ɪnˈvɛnʃən 〕 *n.* 發明

Of all the new *inventions*, cell phones have changed our lives the most.

jam 〔 dʒæm 〕 *n.* 阻塞

Traffic *jams* often waste people's time, and they also produce air pollution.

joke 〔 dʒok 〕 *n.* 笑話

John usually told a *joke* when an embarrassing situation occurred.

kind 〔 kaɪnd 〕 *n.* 種類

Mary is pretty, but she isn't the *kind* of girl I love.

kitchen 〔ˈkɪtʃɪn 〕 *n.* 廚房

Early every morning, my mother fixes breakfast for us in the *kitchen*.

* fix 〔 fɪks 〕 *v.* 準備（飯菜）

自 我 測 驗

- [ ] interest _____
- [ ] ground _____
- [ ] future _____
- [ ] fake _____
- [ ] history _____

- [ ] flight _____
- [ ] invention _____
- [ ] fault _____
- [ ] grade _____
- [ ] kitchen _____

- [ ] finger _____
- [ ] happiness _____
- [ ] factory _____
- [ ] experience _____
- [ ] garbage _____

Check List

1.	過　錯	f	*fault*	t
2.	發　明	i		n
3.	仿冒品	f		e
4.	成　績	g		e
5.	經　驗	e		e
6.	興　趣	i		t
7.	地　面	g		d
8.	班　機	f		t
9.	快　樂	h		s
10.	工　廠	f		y
11.	未　來	f		e
12.	廚　房	k		n
13.	手　指	f		r
14.	歷　史	h		y
15.	垃　圾	g		e

language (ˈlæŋgwɪdʒ) *n.* 語言

If you want to be good at a foreign *language*, you have to practice it.

【典型考題】

English is not my native _____.
(A) subject   (B) language
(C) country   (D) school

答案:**B**

life (laɪf) *n.* 生命

Both her parents lost their *lives* in the accident, so Betty was sent to the orphanage.

* orphanage (ˈɔrfənɪdʒ) *n.* 孤兒院

light (laɪt) *n.* 燈

It is dark inside. Would you please turn on the *light*?

looks (lʊks) *n. pl.* 長相

Don't judge a person by his *looks*.

machine 〔 məˈʃin 〕 *n.* 機器

I wish I could fly to the past in a time *machine* and change history.

meal 〔 mil 〕 *n.* 一餐

Breakfast is a *meal* we should eat every day.

medicine 〔ˈmɛdəsn̩〕 *n.* 藥

Susan had a bad cold yesterday, but she felt much better after taking some *medicine*.

* bad 〔 bæd 〕 *adj.* 嚴重的

【典型考題】

This ＿＿＿＿＿＿ will make you feel better soon.

(A) answer   (B) medicine

(C) fever   (D) headache

答案：**B**

motorcyclist (ˈmotɚˌsaɪklɪst) *n.*

機車騎士

The *motorcyclist* was going too fast when the traffic lights changed to red.

```
motorcycl  +  ist
   |           |
  機車    +   人
```

【典型考題】

The _____ was not hurt in the
traffic accident because he was wearing
a helmet.

(A) pilot   (B) swimmer

(C) car   (D) motorcyclist

答案：**D**

mountain (ˈmaʊntn̩) *n.* 山

On holidays, more and more people
watch birds in the *mountains*.

movie ('muvɪ) *n.* 電影

I'm sorry. I can't go to the *movies* with
you tomorrow.

【典型考題】

I saw a(n) _____ at the theater
yesterday.

(A) movie   (B) experience
(C) speech   (D) popcorn

答案：**A**

MRT 捷運 (= *Mass Rapid Transit*)

In Taipei, it's much faster to go some
places by *MRT* than by car.

museum (mju'ziəm) *n.* 博物館

The best way to help a foreigner
understand Chinese culture is to take
him to a *museum*.

【典型考題】

We went to the ＿＿＿＿＿ to see the
paintings of the famous artist.

(A) grocery store   (B) museum
(C) gas station   (D) hardware store

答案：**B**

neighbor 〔'nebɚ〕 *n.* 鄰居

My *neighbor* intends to throw a farewell
party for me before I go abroad.

* ***throw a party*** 舉行宴會
   farewell party 送別會   ***go abroad*** 出國

newspaper 〔'njuz,pepɚ〕 *n.* 報紙

I saw my teammates' picture in the
newspaper.

noise 〔nɔɪz〕 *n.* 噪音

There's so much *noise* in the street that
I cannot hear you .

nose 〔 noz 〕 *n.* 鼻子

It is sometimes wise to follow your *nose*
and make your own plans.

* wise 〔 waɪz 〕 *adj.* 聰明的
   follow *one's* ***nose*** 憑直覺行事

notice 〔'notɪs 〕 *n.* 海報；公告

I often read *notices* of the latest movies
before I see them.

novel 〔'nɑvl̩ 〕 *n.* 小說

"The Old Man and the Sea" is a great *novel*
that was written by Hemingway.

【典型考題】

I found a good ＿＿＿＿＿ in the bookstore.

(A) radio   (B) calculator

(C) novel   (D) library

答案：**C**

office 〔'ɔfɪs〕 n. 辦公室

I usually call on him at his *office*.

* *call on* 拜訪（某人）

opportunity 〔ˌɑpɚ'tjunətɪ〕 n. 機會

In ancient China, few women were given
the *opportunity* to learn how to read
and write.

* ancient 〔'enʃənt〕 *adj.* 古代的

【典型考題】

Going to university is a good _____
to increase your knowledge.

(A) opportunity   (B) job

(C) study   (D) school

答案：**A**

overpass 〔'ovɚˌpæs 〕 *n.* 天橋

We can take the *overpass* to cross the railway.

* ***take the overpass*** 走天橋
  railway 〔'relˌwe 〕 *n.* 鐵路

painting 〔'pentɪŋ 〕 *n.* 畫

Some people think the *paintings* by Picasso are ugly while others think otherwise.

* ugly 〔'ʌglɪ 〕 *adj.* 醜的
  otherwise 〔'ʌðɚˌwaɪz 〕 *adv.* 不那樣

parents 〔'pɛrənts 〕 *n. pl.* 父母

"Do you live with your father and mother?"

"Yes, I live with my *parents*."

自 我 測 驗

☐ MRT _____

☐ novel _____

☐ opportunity _____

☐ noise _____

☐ museum _____

☐ machine _____

☐ life _____

☐ looks _____

☐ movie _____

☐ painting _____

☐ neighbor _____

☐ parents _____

☐ notice _____

☐ light _____

☐ nose _____

Check List

1. 畫　　　p _____painting_____ g
2. 機　會　o _____ y
3. 長　相　l _____ s
4. 藥　　　m _____ e
5. 山　　　m _____ n

6. 機　器　m _____ e
7. 天　橋　o _____ s
8. 電　影　m _____ e
9. 一　餐　m _____ l
10. 噪　音　n _____ e

11. 公　告　n _____ e
12. 父　母　p _____ s
13. 鄰　居　n _____ r
14. 燈　　　l _____ t
15. 小　說　n _____ l

passenger 〔'pæsṇdʒɚ 〕 *n.* 乘客

In Taipei, over 500,000 *passengers* take the MRT to school or work every day.

【典型考題】

The _____ on the airplane were unhappy with the service.

(A) passengers   (B) skills

(C) wars   (D) tickets

答案：**A**

person 〔'pɝsṇ 〕 *n.* 人

I've talked to my net friend several times, but I've never met her in *person*.

* *net friend* 網友   *in person* 親自

piece 〔 pis 〕 *n.* 一片

Linda cut the cake into four *pieces*.

place 〔 ples 〕 *n.* 地位

Alex is the one whom I love most. No one can take his *place*.

plant 〔 plænt 〕 *n.* 植物

This *plant* will die if you don't give it enough water.

pocket 〔'pɑkɪt〕 *n.* 口袋

Don't stand with your hands in your *pockets*.

pollution 〔 pə'luʃən 〕 *n.* 污染

Heavy traffic will bring us the problem of air *pollution*.

【典型考題】

The factory produces a lot of _____.

(A) air   (B) pollution

(C) workers   (D) sales

答案：**B**

poster〔'postɚ 〕 n. 海報

All the walls of Helen's room are decorated with *posters* of Tom Cruise.

【典型考題】

The _____ on the wall says that there will be a concert on Friday.

(A) radio　　　　　(B) musician
(C) poster　　　　 (D) window

答案：**C**

prescription〔 prɪ'skrɪpʃən 〕 n. 處方

Remember that you can't buy medicine without your doctor's *prescription*.

【典型考題】

The doctor gave me a(n) _____ so that I could buy the medicine.

(A) bill　　　　　　(B) appointment
(C) nurse　　　　　(D) prescription

答案：**D**

present 〔'prɛznt 〕 *n.* 禮物

My son's birthday is coming up. I want to
buy him a computer as a birthday *present*.

【典型考題】

I bought my mother a _____ for
Mother's Day.
(A) child   (B) father
(C) present   (D) Sunday

答案：**C**

price 〔 praɪs 〕 *n.* 價格

Peter wanted to buy that camera, but the
price was too high.

program 〔'progræm 〕 *n.* 計畫

Taiwan needs a good recycling *program*
to deal with the garbage.

* recycling 〔ˌri'saɪklɪŋ 〕 *n.* 回收
   deal with 處理

rate〔 ret 〕*n.* 速度

She can type at the *rate* of 80 words per
minute.

reflector〔 rɪˈflɛktɚ 〕*n.* 反射鏡;反光物

Riding a bicycle with a *reflector* behind
is smart.

roof〔 ruf 〕*n.* 屋頂

People often call Mount Everest the *roof*
of the world.

room〔 rum 〕*n.* 空間

Would you move over and make *room*
for the old lady?

* *make room for* 讓出空位給~

salad 〔'sæləd〕 *n.* 沙拉

Vegetarians will eat *salad*, but they do not eat meat.

seat 〔 sit 〕 *n.* 座位

He took a *seat* next to me.

semester 〔 sə'mɛstɚ 〕 *n.* 學期

I can't believe this is our last *semester*; we are leaving school in a few weeks.

sentence 〔'sɛntəns〕 *n.* 句子

Try to make a *sentence* like the one in the book.

【典型考題】

How many _____ are there in this paragraph?

(A) writers   (B) sentences

(C) homework   (D) titles

答案：**B**

September ﹝ sɛpˈtɛmbɚ ﹞ *n.* 九月

In Taiwan, the first semester of the school year usually begins in *September*.

shortcut ﹝ˈʃɔrtˌkʌt ﹞ *n.* 捷徑

There is no *shortcut* to learning.

side ﹝ saɪd ﹞ *n.* 邊；面

I must have got up on the wrong *side* of the bed this morning! Nothing seemed to go right today.

* ***get up on the wrong side of the bed*** 心情不好
go right 順利

sky ﹝ skaɪ ﹞ *n.* 天空

It is said that we can make a wish on a falling star we see in the night *sky*.

software ('sɔft,wɛr) *n.* 軟體

I just bought some computer *software* that can draw various kinds of pictures.

* various ('vɛrɪəs) *adj.* 各式各樣的

【典型考題】

The programmer writes computer _____ for a living.

(A) e-mail   (B) Internet

(C) hardware   (D) software

答案：**D**

space (spes) *n.* 太空

It's amazing in outer *space*.

* amazing (ə'mezɪŋ) *adj.* 令人驚奇的

   outer space 太空

sport (sport) *n.* 運動

I enjoy playing *sports*, and it makes me healthier.

🐭 自 我 測 驗

- [ ] person   _____
- [ ] piece   _____
- [ ] roof   _____
- [ ] space   _____
- [ ] program   _____

- [ ] passenger   _____
- [ ] poster   _____
- [ ] plant   _____
- [ ] present   _____
- [ ] pocket   _____

- [ ] reflector   _____
- [ ] prescription   _____
- [ ] sentence   _____
- [ ] semester   _____
- [ ] pollution   _____

Check List

1. 座　位　s ___seat___ t
2. 人　　　p _____ n
3. 屋　頂　r _____ f
4. 太　空　s _____ e
5. 價　格　p _____ e

6. 學　期　s _____ r
7. 海　報　p _____ r
8. 處　方　p _____ n
9. 污　染　p _____ n
10. 植　物　p _____ t

11. 禮　物　p _____ t
12. 反光物　r _____ r
13. 句　子　s _____ e
14. 乘　客　p _____ r
15. 一　片　p _____ e

steak 〔 stek 〕 n. 牛排

After I finished my *steak*, the waiter
gave me the dessert.

step 〔 stεp 〕 n. 步

Don't be afraid. The first *step* is always
the hardest. All you have to do is try
your best.

* ***all one has to do is + V.*** 某人必須做的是

stranger 〔'strendʒɚ 〕 n. 陌生人

She is a *stranger* to me.

【典型考題】

I saw a(n) ＿＿＿＿＿＿ go into the house
and called the police.

(A) spider   (B) stranger
(C) uncle   (D) giant

答案：**B**

subject (ˈsʌbdʒɪkt) *n.* 科目

Of all these *subjects*, I like Chinese best.

success (səkˈsɛs) *n.* 成功

It goes without saying that hard work brings *success*.

* ***it goes without saying that*** ~ 不用說，~

sweater (ˈswɛtɚ) *n.* 毛衣

When it is cold, Mother asks me to wear a *sweater* when I go out.

system (ˈsɪstəm) *n.* 系統

The MRT *system* makes our life much more convenient than before.

talent 〔'tælənt 〕 *n.* 才能；天份

Cathy has a special *talent* for music.

She can play the piano very well.

【典型考題】

Playing the flute well is just one of his

_____.

(A) talents   (B) works

(C) uses   (D) cases

答案：**A**

team 〔 tim 〕 *n.* 隊

Soccer is a kind of *team* sport. That means you cannot play it by yourself.

theater 〔'θiətɚ 〕 *n.* 電影院；戲院

Each of the *theaters* always has a different movie.

tip 〔 tɪp 〕 *n.* 秘訣

How did you learn English so well?

Can you offer me some *tips*?

【典型考題】

He gave me some _____ that helped me pass the test.

(A) money   (B) tips

(C) fruit   (D) teachers

答案：**B**

tool 〔 tul 〕 *n.* 工具

A dictionary is a very useful *tool* in learning languages.

touch 〔 tʌtʃ 〕 *n.* 接觸

After leaving, I hope we can stay in *touch*.

traffic 〔'træfɪk 〕 *n.* 交通

In many big cities, the serious *traffic* problem needs to be solved soon.

【典型考題】

There is always a lot of _____ during rush hour (尖峰時間) .

(A) traffic   (B) time

(C) accidents   (D) neighbors

答案：**A**

train 〔 tren 〕 n. 火車

I have to get to the station, because my *train* leaves in half an hour.

trouble 〔ˈtrʌbḷ〕 n. 麻煩

If I told you the truth, I'd get into a lot of *trouble*.

truth 〔 truθ 〕 n. 事實

I thought the radio was broken. The *truth* is I forgot to plug it in.

* *plug in* 插上插頭；接通電源

twenty-one 〔'twεntɪ'wʌn 〕 *n.* 二十一

In some countries it is illegal for people
to buy alcohol before the age of
twenty-one.

twins 〔 twɪnz 〕 *n. pl.* 雙胞胎

John and Peter are *twins* . When you see
them, you can't tell who is who.

【典型考題】

Of course the _____ have the same
birthday.
(A) books (B) twins
(C) schools (D) cakes

答案：**B**

typhoon 〔 taɪ'fun 〕 *n.* 颱風

All communication has been cut off by
the big *typhoon*.

umbrella 〔ʌmˈbrɛlə〕 *n.* 雨傘

It looks like rain. Why not take an *umbrella* with you?

【典型考題】

That firm can advertise all kinds of products such as clothes, shoes or _____.

(A) trousers   (B) T-shirts
(C) umbrellas   (D) sports shoes

答案：**C**

vacation 〔veˈkeʃən〕 *n.* 假期

Winter *vacation* usually starts in January or February.

【典型考題】

We will have a two-week _____ in winter during which we won't have to go to school.

(A) umbrella   (B) homework
(C) vacation   (D) semester

答案：**C**

vendor ('vɛndə) *n.* 小販

I bought this pair of glasses from a street *vendor* last week.

village ('vɪlɪdʒ) *n.* 村莊

Because communication has become so easy and convenient, the world is like a small *village*.

voice (vɔɪs) *n.* 聲音

I heard the children's *voices* at the back of the house.

wallet ('wɑlɪt) *n.* 皮夾

When he had to pay the bill, he couldn't find his *wallet*. He felt embarrassed.

☜ 自 我 測 驗

☐ step _____

☐ wallet _____

☐ team _____

☐ talent _____

☐ umbrella _____

☐ voice _____

☐ success _____

☐ village _____

☐ subject _____

☐ vendor _____

☐ truth _____

☐ typhoon _____

☐ traffic _____

☐ sweater _____

☐ vacation _____

🐭 Check List

1. 才　能　t_____talent_____ t
2. 聲　音　v_____ e
3. 工　具　t_____ l
4. 麻　煩　t_____ e
5. 村　落　v_____ e

6. 科　目　s_____ t
7. 皮　夾　w_____ t
8. 雨　傘　u_____ a
9. 小　販　v_____ r
10. 雙胞胎　t_____ s

11. 假　期　v_____ n
12. 事　實　t_____ h
13. 颱　風　t_____ n
14. 交　通　t_____ c
15. 接　觸　t_____ h

way 〔 we 〕 *n.* 道路;方向

Don't get in my *way*! I can't see the TV!

* ***get in*** *one's* ***way*** 擋某人的路;妨礙某人

【典型考題】

Would you please show me the _____
to the train station?

(A) weed   (B) way

(C) watch   (D) sign

答案:**B**

wind 〔 wɪnd 〕 *n.* 風

Jack runs like the *wind*. He runs faster
than any other student in his school.

【典型考題】

The _____ is so strong that I can't move
a step.

(A) wind   (B) body

(C) pie   (D) wish

答案:**A**

window 〔'wɪndo 〕*n.* 窗戶

It is so hot inside. Can you open the
window for me?

【典型考題】

Remember to close the _____; it
might rain.

(A) roof   (B) window
(C) book   (D) umbrella

答案：**B**

wish 〔 wɪʃ 〕*n.* 願望

She closed her eyes and made a *wish*.

youth 〔 juθ 〕*n.* 年輕人

Jack is a *youth* of twenty.

zoo 〔 zu 〕*n.* 動物園

My parents like to bring us to the *zoo* on
holidays.

動 詞

act 〔 ækt 〕 v. 行動

We *acted* on his orders.

* order 〔'ɔrdə 〕 n. 命令

add 〔 æd 〕 v. 增加

She tasted her coffee and *added* some
more sugar.

* taste 〔 test 〕 v. 品嚐   sugar 〔'suɡə 〕 n. 糖

advise 〔 əd'vaɪz 〕 v. 勸告

I *advised* my father not to smoke too much.

【典型考題】

I _____ that he should not drink too much.

(A) advised   (B) quitted

(C) stopped   (D) kept

答案：**A**

affect 〔ə'fɛkt〕 v. 影響

Doctors say that smoking *affects* health.

【典型考題】

He was much _____ by the news.

(A) afforded
(B) affected
(C) acted
(D) added

答案：**B**

afford 〔ə'ford〕 v. 負擔得起

I can't *afford* such an expensive car.

【典型考題】

You spent too much money. How can you _____ the expense?

(A) relieve
(B) receive
(C) affect
(D) afford

答案：**D**

allow 〔 ə'laʊ 〕 *v.* 允許

Her parents didn't *allow* her to go to the U.S.

answer 〔'ænsɚ 〕 *v.* 回答

Answer my question. Don't be silent.

【典型考題】

It's not easy to _____ the difficult question.

(A) answer   (B) tell

(C) say   (D) speak

答案：**A**

apologize 〔 ə'pɑlə,dʒaɪz 〕 *v.* 道歉

Ken *apologized* to his girlfriend for forgetting the date.

* date 〔 det 〕 *n.* 約會

arrive 〔 ə'raɪv 〕 *v.* 到達

Can you *arrive* here on time?

* *on time* 準時

ask 〔 æsk 〕 v. 問

You can *ask* a question of your teacher.

【典型考題】

What a fool you are to _____ such a
stupid question!

(A) treat   (B) ask

(C) reach   (D) live

答案：**B**

attend 〔 ə'tɛnd 〕 v. 參加；出席

"Will you *attend* the party tonight?"

"Yes, I was invited."

avoid 〔 ə'vɔɪd 〕 v. 避免

You had better *avoid* dark streets in New
York if you don't want to be robbed.

* rob 〔 rɑb 〕 v. 搶劫

【典型考題】

_____ crossing this street at rush hours.

(A) Finish   (B) Invite

(C) Avoid   (D) Invent

答案：**C**

bark 〔 bɑrk 〕 *v.* 吠叫

Our dog always *barks* at strangers.

beat 〔 bit 〕 *v.* 打

Be quiet, or I'll *beat* you black and blue.

* quiet 〔 kwaɪət 〕 *adj.* 安靜的

  beat sb. black and blue 把某人打得鼻青臉腫

become 〔 bɪ'kʌm 〕 *v.* 變得

Long time no see. You *become* more beautiful every year.

begin 〔 bɪ'gɪn 〕 v. 開始

We *begin* our class at 8:00 every morning.

【典型考題】

"When did you _____ to learn English?"
"When I was ten years old."

(A) sleep   (B) watch

(C) keep   (D) begin

答案：**D**

believe 〔 bɪ'liv 〕 v. 相信

I can't *believe* it! You have eaten
them all.

【典型考題】

You should always do what you _____
to be right.

(A) raise   (B) truth

(C) truth   (D) believe

答案：**D**

- [ ] beat _____
- [ ] advise _____
- [ ] believe _____
- [ ] youth _____
- [ ] apologize _____

- [ ] attend _____
- [ ] bark _____
- [ ] become _____
- [ ] way _____
- [ ] window _____

- [ ] arrive _____
- [ ] attend _____
- [ ] wind _____
- [ ] wish _____
- [ ] affect _____

Check List

1. 打	b	_beat_	t
2. 勸 告	a		e
3. 相 信	b		e
4. 年輕人	y		h
5. 道 歉	a		e
6. 參 加	a		d
7. 吠 叫	b		k
8. 變 得	b		e
9. 道 路	w		y
10. 窗 戶	w		w
11. 到 達	a		e
12. 出 席	a		d
13. 風	w		d
14. 願 望	w		h
15. 影 響	a		t

bite 〔 baɪt 〕 v. 咬

When I was a boy, the neighbor's dog *bit*
me and hurt my leg.

blame 〔 blem 〕 v. 責備

It's my fault. I'm to *blame*.

* *be to blame* 該受責備

bleed 〔 blid 〕 v. 流血

Your nose is *bleeding*. What's wrong?

boil 〔 bɔɪl 〕 v. 煮沸

Please *boil* some water. I want to make
some coffee.

* *make coffee* 泡咖啡

book 〔 bʊk 〕 v. 預訂

I have *booked* a seat on a plane to Taipei.

* plane 〔 plen 〕 n. 飛機

borrow 〔'bɑro 〕v. 借 (入)

Susan wants to *borrow* the book when you're done with it.

* *be done with* 看完

【典型考題】

I have _____ this bicycle from Henry.

(A) lent   (B) kicked

(C) borrowed   (D) boiled

答案：**C**

bother 〔'bɑðɚ 〕v. 麻煩

Don't *bother*. I'm leaving.

break 〔 brek 〕v. 折斷

Sandra *broke* her leg last night.

【典型考題】

The shot _____ the peace of the morning.

(A) broken   (B) bit

(C) broke   (D) built

答案：**C**

build 〔 bɪld 〕 *v.* 建造

He has *built* his parents a new house.

【典型考題】

I like to live in a house ＿＿＿＿＿ of wood.

(A) bought 　　　　(B) built

(C) burst 　　　　　(D) bump

答案：**B**

bump 〔 bʌmp 〕 *v.* 撞到

Don't worry about me. I just *bumped* against the desk.

【典型考題】

On my way home, I ＿＿＿＿＿ into a classmate from elementary school.

(A) happened 　　　　(B) hit

(C) bumped 　　　　(D) borrowed

答案：**C**

buy 〔 baɪ 〕 v. 買

Yesterday I *bought* a dress for my daughter as her birthday present.

【典型考題】

My father _____ a vase for 10,000 dollars.

(A) bought   (B) caught

(C) thought   (D) lighted

答案：**A**

call 〔 kɔl 〕 v. 打電話給~

Don't forget to *call* me up after you get there.

* *call sb. up* 打電話給某人

camp 〔 kæmp 〕 v. 露營

We will go *camping* in the mountains this weekend.

care〔kɛr〕v. 在乎

I don't *care* if I fail. I will do my best.

* *do one's best* 盡力

catch〔kætʃ〕v. 接（球）；捕捉

My dog is very smart. It can *catch* a ball.

* smart〔smɑrt〕*adj.* 聰明的

celebrate〔'sɛlə,bret〕v. 慶祝

If our plan works, we will *celebrate* in a special way.

* work〔wɝk〕*v.* 行得通
  in one's *way* 以～方式

【典型考題】

Christmas Day is _____ on December 25 in the West.

(A) bought (B) took
(C) caught (D) celebrated

答案：**D**

choose 〔 tʃuz 〕 *v.* 選擇

Adam was very disappointed about not being *chosen* for the soccer team.

* disappointed (ˌdɪsəˈpɔɪntɪd) *adj.* 失望的

clean 〔 klin 〕 *v.* 打掃

I must *clean* my room.

clear 〔 klɪr 〕 *v.* 清理

I often help Mother *clear* up my room on Sunday.

complain 〔 kəmˈplen 〕 *v.* 抱怨

Can you keep the children quiet? Our neighbors are *complaining* about the noise.

concentrate 〔'kɑnsn̩‚tret 〕 v. 專心

You can't *concentrate* on your studies if you watch TV while doing your homework.

【典型考題】

He _____ on driving the jeep.

(A) concentrated (B) communicated
(C) climbed (D) congratulated

答案：**A**

control 〔 kən'trol 〕 v. 控制

The government *controls* the price of rice.

* government 〔'gʌvə·nmənt 〕 n. 政府
  price 〔 praɪs 〕 n. 價格   rice 〔 raɪs 〕 n. 稻米

【典型考題】

Everyone is supposed to _____ his temper.

(A) repeat (B) laugh
(C) control (D) choose

答案：**C**

copy 〔'kɑpɪ 〕v. 抄襲

He always asked me to let him *copy* my
math homework.

create 〔 krɪ'et 〕v. 創造

New words are *created*, and some old
words develop new meanings.
* develop 〔 dɪ'vɛləp 〕v. 發展

【典型考題】

The writer _____ his own stories.
(A) creates   (B) listens
(C) watches   (D) builds

答案：**A**

criticize 〔'krɪtə,saɪz 〕v. 批評

Don't *criticize* your friends in front of
them, because it will make them
uncomfortable.

自 我 測 驗

- [ ] bump　　　　　_____
- [ ] criticize　　　_____
- [ ] bleed　　　　 _____
- [ ] control　　　 _____
- [ ] bother　　　　_____

- [ ] concentrate　_____
- [ ] break　　　　 _____
- [ ] complain　　 _____
- [ ] build　　　　 _____
- [ ] choose　　　 _____

- [ ] blame　　　　_____
- [ ] create　　　　_____
- [ ] buy　　　　　 _____
- [ ] celebrate　　 _____
- [ ] camp　　　　 _____

Check List

1. 買　　　　b _____buy_____ y
2. 批　評　　c _____ e
3. 控　制　　c _____ l
4. 慶　祝　　c _____ e
5. 撞　到　　b _____ p

6. 責　備　　b _____ e
7. 麻　煩　　b _____ r
8. 建　造　　b _____ d
9. 選　擇　　c _____ e
10. 抱　怨　　c _____ n

11. 專　心　　c _____ e
12. 創　造　　c _____ e
13. 折　斷　　b _____ k
14. 流　血　　b _____ d
15. 露　營　　c _____ p

decide 〔 dɪˈsaɪd 〕 v. 決定

After thinking for a long time, he *decided* not to buy the car.

【典型考題】

She couldn't _____ which way to go.

(A) drive   (B) decide

(C) look   (D) touch

答案：**B**

decorate 〔ˈdɛkəˌret 〕 v. 裝飾

To celebrate Christmas, Americans usually *decorate* Christmas trees with lights.

* light 〔 laɪt 〕 n. 燈

【典型考題】

The room was _____ with an old picture.

(A) decorated   (B) decided

(C) landed   (D) seated

答案：**A**

develop〔dɪˈvɛləp〕v. 培養

Our teacher encourages us to do activities which help *develop* a strong body .

* encourage〔ɪnˈkɝɪdʒ〕v. 鼓勵
  activity〔ækˈtɪvətɪ〕n. 活動

die〔daɪ〕v. 死去；消失

My love for you has *died*. Let's break up.

* *break up* 分手

differ〔ˈdɪfɚ〕v. 不同

My dress *differs* from yours.

dislike〔dɪsˈlaɪk〕v. 不喜歡

Do you *dislike* doing housework?

* housework〔ˈhaʊsˌwɝk〕n. 家事

divorce 〔dəˈvors〕v. 離婚

The couple didn't get along well, so they decided to *divorce*.

* couple 〔ˈkʌpḷ〕n. 夫妻   *get along* 相處

do 〔du〕v. 做

Students are to *do* their homework every day.

draw 〔drɔ〕v. 畫

I *drew* a picture of my mother and gave it to her as a Mother's Day present.

【典型考題】

He _____ a straight line between our seats to show we had "broken up."

(A) wrote   (B) applied

(C) drew   (D) did

答案：**C**

drink ﹝ drɪŋk ﹞ v. 喝

People like to *drink* iced drinks on hot summer days.

* iced ﹝ aɪst ﹞ *adj.* 冰的

drive ﹝ draɪv ﹞ v. 開車

My father *drives* a car to work, so he never takes the MRT.

earn ﹝ ɝn ﹞ v. 賺

How much do you *earn* every month?

* month ﹝ mʌnθ ﹞ *n.* 月

【典型考題】

Mary _____ money by teaching.

(A) eases   (B) harms

(C) earns   (D) delivers

答案：**C**

end〔ɛnd〕v. 結束

Our summer vacation *ends* in September.

enjoy〔ɪn'dʒɔɪ〕v. 喜歡

I *enjoy* reading novels in my free time.

* novel〔'nɑvḷ〕n. 小說　*free time* 空閒時間

【典型考題】

Did you ＿＿＿＿＿ your trip?
(A) enter　　　　　(B) enjoy
(C) break　　　　　(D) follow

答案：**B**

enter〔'ɛntɚ〕v. 進入；參加

He *entered* the classroom.

【典型考題】

I decided to ＿＿＿＿＿ the contest.
(A) jump　　　　　(B) enter
(C) rush　　　　　(D) earn

答案：**B**

examine ﹝ ɪgˊzæmɪn ﹞ v. 檢查

After the doctor *examined* my eyes carefully, he told me I needed a pair of glasses.

* pair ﹝ pɛr ﹞ n. 一副；一對

fill ﹝ fɪl ﹞ v. 裝滿

Fill the bottle with water, please.

find ﹝ faɪnd ﹞ v. 找到

Please help me. I can't *find* my wallet.

finish ﹝ ˊfɪnɪʃ ﹞ v. 完成

I haven't *finished* my homework. May I copy yours?

fit ﹝ fɪt ﹞ v. 適合

The shoes don't *fit* me. I need another pair.

fix 〔 fɪks 〕 *v.* 修理

My radio doesn't work. I have to get someone to *fix* it.

* work 〔 wɜk 〕 *v.* 運作

follow 〔'fɑlo 〕 *v.* 遵循

Please *follow* these tips, and you'll do well on all the tests.

* *do well* 考得好

forget 〔 fɚ'gɛt 〕 *v.* 忘記

I often *forget* to take the medicine on time.

gain 〔 gen 〕 *v.* 增加

I *gained* five kilos in weight.

* weight 〔 wet 〕 *n.* 體重

graduate ('grædʒu,et) v. 畢業

I made up my mind to be a PE teacher after I *graduated* from school.

* ***make up** one's **mind*** 下定決心

  PE 體育 (= *physical education*)

greet (grit) v. 打招呼

Remember to *greet* your teachers and classmates every morning.

grow (gro) v. 生長

Does this fruit *grow* in warm places?

【典型考題】

I ＿＿＿＿＿ up in the country and enjoyed the fresh air there.

(A) grew (B) jumped
(C) pushed (D) looked

答案：**A**

☐ fit _____

☐ do _____

☐ end _____

☐ fix _____

☐ grow _____

☐ gain _____

☐ die _____

☐ enter _____

☐ earn _____

☐ differ _____

☐ draw _____

☐ enjoy _____

☐ fill _____

☐ drive _____

☐ dislike _____

Check List

1. 找　到　f _____ *find* _____ d
2. 決　定　d _____ e
3. 離　婚　d _____ e
4. 完　成　f _____ h
5. 檢　查　e _____ e

6. 裝　飾　d _____ e
7. 遵　循　f _____ w
8. 畢　業　g _____ e
9. 忘　記　f _____ t
10. 培　養　d _____ p

11. 喝　　　d _____ k
12. 打招呼　g _____ t
13. 開　車　d _____ e
14. 進　入　e _____ r
15. 適　合　f _____ t

hand 〔 hænd 〕 v. 交給～

My father *handed* me a piece of paper this morning.

harm 〔 hɑrm 〕 v. 傷害

Don't read in too strong or weak light, because it may *harm* your eyes.

help 〔 hɛlp 〕 v. 幫忙

Please *help* me carry this box upstairs.

【典型考題】

I often ＿＿＿＿ my classmate with his math homework.

(A) have   (B) eat

(C) forget   (D) help

答案：**D**

hug 〔 hʌg 〕 v. 擁抱

They are *hugging* to say goodbye to each other.

hunt 〔 hʌnt 〕 v. 打獵

My father likes to go *hunting* in his spare time.

hurry 〔 'hɜɪ 〕 v. 趕快

We have to *hurry*; the movie *Cats & Dogs* will begin in five minutes.

hurt 〔 hɜt 〕 v. 使受傷

What Mike said to me *hurt* my feelings, but I guess I can forgive him this time.

【典型考題】

Many people were _____ in the train accident.

(A) brought (B) held
(C) hurt (D) lose

答案：**C**

imagine 〔 ɪ'mædʒɪn 〕 v. 想像

Try to *imagine* that you're traveling in space.

invent 〔 ɪn'vɛnt 〕 v. 發明

Alexander Graham Bell *invented* the world's first telephone.

jam 〔 dʒæm 〕 v. 塞滿；擁擠 *n.* 果醬

During the big sale, the department store is always *jammed* with people.

jog 〔 dʒɑg 〕 v. 慢跑

You can see many people *jogging* in the park every evening.

jump 〔 dʒʌmp 〕 v. 跳

I like to *jump* rope.

keep 〔 kip 〕 *v.* 保持

Mom told me to *keep* my room clean all the time.

【典型考題】

Would you please _____ quiet for a while?

(A) keep   (B) jump

(C) hit   (D) ride

答案：**A**

kill 〔 kɪl 〕 *v.* 消磨（時間）

I looked at the CDs in a music store in order to *kill* time.

leave 〔 liv 〕 *v.* 離開

I'm *leaving* for Liverpool on Monday.

lend 〔 lɛnd 〕 *v.* 借（出）

Would you mind *lending* me your pen for a while?

let 〔 lɛt 〕 *v.* 讓

Open the window to *let* in the fresh air.

【典型考題】

Fred's father doesn't ＿＿＿＿ him drive on
weekdays.

(A) give   (B) hope

(C) want   (D) let

答案：**D**

lick 〔 lɪk 〕 *v.* 舔

My cat *licked* my hand, which tickled me.

link 〔 lɪŋk 〕 *v.* 連結

The road *links* the two villages.

lock 〔 lɑk 〕 *v.* 鎖上

He *locked* up the jewels before going
away.

lose〔luz〕v. 失去

Don't *lose* your temper, Jim. I was only trying to give you some friendly advice.

【典型考題】

When he ＿＿＿＿＿ his sight he had to stop his research work.

(A) lost (B) loss
(C) losing (D) lose

答案：**A**

make〔mek〕v. 賺（錢）

Jim needs to *make* some money to be able to take a trip to New York this summer.

【典型考題】

Inventing new things will ＿＿＿＿＿ a lot of money.

(A) cut (B) dig
(C) make (D) hug

答案：**C**

match 〔 mætʃ 〕 v. 搭配

The shoes do not *match* your dress.

meet 〔 mit 〕 v. 符合

It took me more time to finish the report, so I couldn't *meet* the deadline.

mind 〔 maɪnd 〕 v. 介意

It's really hot in here. Do you *mind* if I open a window?

【典型考題】

I don't _____ you smoking here.

(A) mad   (B) mind

(C) mean   (D) make

答案：**B**

mop 〔 mɑp 〕 v. 拖（地）

When the floor is dirty, my brother is always the first one to *mop* it.

move 〔 muv 〕 v. 移動

The wind *moved* the branches of the trees.

notice 〔'notɪs 〕 v. 注意到

Did you *notice* that Amy's been a little too quiet these days?

open 〔'opən 〕 v. 打開

Mother taught me that it's impolite to *open* a gift in front of others.

pack 〔 pæk 〕 v. 打包

Mark is *packing* now because he will go on a trip.

park 〔 pɑrk 〕 v. 停車

He *parked* his car next to the house.

自我測驗

- [ ] lock   _____
- [ ] hug   _____
- [ ] lose   _____
- [ ] mop   _____
- [ ] open   _____

- [ ] help   _____
- [ ] move   _____
- [ ] mind   _____
- [ ] hand   _____
- [ ] hunt   _____

- [ ] jog   _____
- [ ] keep   _____
- [ ] let   _____
- [ ] make   _____
- [ ] harm   _____

Check List

1. 塞　滿　　j _____ *jam* _____ m

2. 離　開　　l _____ e

3. 連　結　　l _____ k

4. 搭　配　　m _____ h

5. 打　包　　p _____ k

6. 跳　　　　j _____ p

7. 發　明　　i _____ t

8. 趕　快　　h _____ y

9. 想　像　　i _____ e

10. 借（出）　l _____ d

11. 舔　　　　l _____ k

12. 注　意　　n _____ e

13. 停　車　　p _____ k

14. 介　意　　m _____ d

15. 傷　害　　h _____ m

pay 〔 pe 〕 v. 付錢

Who is going to *pay* the bill?

practice 〔'præktɪs 〕 v. 練習

If you want to play soccer well, you need *practice* it a little more.

【典型考題】

You should _____ speaking English more regularly.

(A) practice   (B) dream

(C) exercise   (D) avoid

答案：**A**

praise 〔 prez 〕 v. 讚美

Teresa has a talent for painting. Everyone *praises* her work.

* work 〔 wɜk 〕 n. 作品

prepare 〔 prɪˈpɛr 〕 *v.* 準備

Hope for the best and *prepare* for the worst.

【典型考題】

Students are _____ for the examination.

(A) preparing   (B) running

(C) using   (D) acting

答案：**A**

pretend 〔 prɪˈtɛnd 〕 *v.* 假裝

Although she had just had an argument with her boyfriend, Mary *pretended* everything was fine when her friend called.

* argument 〔ˈɑrgjəmənt〕 *n.* 爭論

produce 〔 prəˈdjus 〕 *v.* 製造

Heavy traffic will *produce* serious air pollution.

* heavy 〔ˈhɛvɪ〕 *adj.* （交通）繁忙的

  pollution 〔pəˈluʃən〕 *n.* 污染

【典型考題】

The musical has _____ a great
sensation.

(A) appeared   (B) moved

(C) produced   (D) pretended

答案：**C**

pronounce〔prə'naʊns〕v. 發音

The letter "h" is not *pronounced* in the
word "honest."

* letter〔'lɛtə〕n. 字母

  honest〔'ɑnɪst〕adj. 誠實的

protect〔prə'tɛkt〕v. 保護

We are supposed to *protect* the wildlife
that is in danger.

* *be supposed to* 應該

  wildlife〔'waɪld,laɪf〕n. 野生動植物

  in danger 瀕臨危險的

quit 〔 kwɪt 〕 v. 戒除

The doctor suggested that my father *quit* smoking.

rain 〔 ren 〕 v. 下雨

Michael had an accident because it *rained* so heavily that he didn't see the oncoming car.

* ***rain heavily*** 下大雨

　　oncoming 〔 ˈɑnˌkʌmɪŋ 〕 *adj.* 迎面而來的

【典型考題】

It never ＿＿＿＿＿ but it pours.

(A) praises　　　　(B) shows

(C) shines　　　　(D) rains

答案：**D**

reach 〔 ritʃ 〕 v. 到達

London can be *reached* in two hours.

read 〔 rid 〕 v. 閱讀

My father usually *reads* the newspaper
after dinner.

【典型考題】

I make it a rule to _____ an English
newspaper every day.

(A) write   (B) kick
(C) read   (D) listen

答案：C

realize 〔'riə,laɪz 〕 v. 了解

They finally *realized* how lucky they were.

relax 〔 rɪ'læks 〕 v. 放鬆

I'm working too hard these days.
I should take a vacation and just *relax*.

* *these days* 最近
  take a vacation 渡假

report 〔 rɪˈport 〕 v. 報告

Any change should be *reported* immediately.

* change 〔 tʃendʒ 〕 n. 改變
  immediately 〔 ɪˈmidɪɪtlɪ 〕 adv. 立刻

return 〔 rɪˈtɜn 〕 v. 回來

We expect him to *return* next Monday.

* expect 〔 ɪkˈspɛkt 〕 v. 預料

review 〔 rɪˈvju 〕 v. 複習

Miss Young asks us to *review* the lessons after class.

【典型考題】

The teacher reminded us to _____ today's lesson.

(A) relax　　　　(B) preview

(C) review　　　(D) forget

答案：**C**

ring 〔 rɪŋ 〕 *v.* 按（鈴）

Someone is *ringing* the bell. Go answer the door!

* bell 〔 bɛl 〕 *n.* 鈴   *answer the door* 應門

save 〔 sev 〕 *v.* 節省；拯救

Make a list before you go shopping if you want to *save* time.

* list 〔 lɪst 〕 *n.* 清單

【典型考題】

The doctor _____ the child's life.
(A) saved   (B) pushed
(C) hurt   (D) complained

答案：**A**

sell 〔 sɛl 〕 *v.* 賣

He *sold* his camera for 20,000 dollars.

send ﹝ sɛnd ﹞ v. 寄;送

He *sent* me a letter of appreciation.

* appreciation ﹝ ə͵prɪʃɪ'eʃən ﹞ n. 感激

serve ﹝ sɜv ﹞ v. 供應

The restaurant *served* a new kind of
dessert today.

set ﹝ sɛt ﹞ v. 設定

We should *set* goals and try to achieve
them.

sing ﹝ sɪŋ ﹞ v. 唱

Fred : That was a great song! Who
　　　　sang it?

Jean : Arnie did. He's my favorite
　　　　singer.

自 我 測 驗

- [ ] set _____
- [ ] pay _____
- [ ] read _____
- [ ] rain _____
- [ ] quit _____

- [ ] relax _____
- [ ] sell _____
- [ ] sing _____
- [ ] ring _____
- [ ] report _____

- [ ] reach _____
- [ ] produce _____
- [ ] praise _____
- [ ] return _____
- [ ] send _____

Check List

1. 保　護　p ___protect___ t
2. 供　應　s _____ e
3. 練　習　p _____ e
4. 假　裝　p _____ d
5. 發　音　p _____ e

6. 了　解　r _____ e
7. 複　習　r _____ w
8. 節　省　s _____ e
9. 準　備　p _____ e
10. 讚　美　p _____ e

11. 放　鬆　r _____ x
12. 製　造　p _____ e
13. 到　達　r _____ h
14. 戒　除　q _____ t
15. 拯　救　s _____ e

smoke〔smok〕 *v.* 抽煙

My father has cut out *smoking*.

* *cut out* 戒除

solve〔salv〕 *v.* 解決

Nobody has ever *solved* the mystery.

* mystery〔'mɪstrɪ〕 *n.* 謎；奧秘

【典型考題】

It's difficult to _____ the housing
problem at present.

(A) deal　　　　　(B) solve
(C) print　　　　　(D) decide

答案：**B**

sour〔saʊr〕 *v.* 變酸

Milk *sours* quickly when the weather
is hot.

speak〔spik〕v. 說

Helen is willing to talk to foreigners, so she *speaks* English well.

* willing〔'wɪlɪŋ〕 *adj.* 願意的
  foreigner〔'fɔrɪnɚ〕 *n.* 外國人

spread〔sprɛd〕v. 鋪

Judy *spread* a cloth on the table.

* cloth〔klɔθ〕 *n.* 布

【典型考題】

In less than 10 years the city has _____ quickly to the east.

(A) spread   (B) spoken

(C) solved   (D) practiced

答案：**A**

surprise〔sə'praɪz〕v. 使驚訝

He sometimes *surprises* us with a sudden visit.

take 〔 tek 〕 *v.* 帶

John is an active language learner. He
always *takes* a dictionary with him.

* active 〔'æktɪv 〕 *adj.* 主動的；積極的

taste 〔 test 〕 *v.* 嚐起來

He *tasted* both cakes and decided neither
was delicious.

* decide 〔 dɪ'saɪd 〕 *v.* 判定
  neither 〔'niðɚ 〕 *pron.* 兩者皆不

teach 〔 titʃ 〕 *v.* 敎

Mr. Wu has *taught* math for twenty-five
years. He has a lot of experience.

【典型考題】

The first thing I'll ＿＿＿＿＿ you is how
to protect yourself.

(A) read   (B) pay
(C) taste   (D) teach

答案：**D**

tell 〔 tɛl 〕 v. 告訴

John didn't know how to *tell* his wife that he had lost his job.

touch 〔 tʌtʃ 〕 v. 碰觸

Some people are not used to being *touched*.

tow 〔 to 〕 v. 拖

There is no parking here. Your car has been *towed* away.

* park 〔 pɑrk 〕 v. 停車

【典型考題】

The car broke down and we had to have it _____.

(A) answered   (B) corrected

(C) towed   (D) built

答案：C

travel ('trævl̩) *v.* 行進；旅行

"How did you know I got fired?"

"Well, bad news *travels* fast."

* fire〔faɪr 〕*v.* 解僱

treat〔 trit 〕*v.* 請客

Today is your birthday. I'll *treat* you to dinner tonight.

try〔 traɪ 〕*v.* 嘗試

That dress is a little too long. Why don't you *try* one in a smaller size?

【典型考題】

_____ this cheese cake and tell me what you think of it.

(A) Speak   (B) Spread

(C) Use   (D) Try

答案：**D**

use 〔 juz 〕 *v.* 使用

Modern people *use* the computer to send e-mail.

vacuum 〔'vækjʊəm 〕 *v.* 用吸塵器打掃

To clean my room, first I *vacuum* the floor and then mop it.

volunteer 〔ˌvɑlən'tɪr 〕 *v.* 自願

Mary *volunteered* to help the patients in the hospital. No one asked her to do so.

* patient 〔'peʃənt 〕 *n.* 病人

  hospital 〔'hɑspɪtl̩ 〕 *n.* 醫院

【典型考題】

If no one else will do the job, then I will
_____ to do it.

(A) volunteer (B) tell

(C) vacuum (D) order

答案：**A**

wash〔 wɑʃ 〕*v.* 洗

Do you help your mother *wash* dishes after dinner?

waste〔 west 〕*v.* 浪費

Don't *waste* your time asking her to change her mind. She'll never listen.

* ***change** one's **mind*** 改變心意

【典型考題】

If you don't make a plan, you will just _____ your time.

(A) count (B) waste

(C) cost (D) save

答案：**B**

watch〔 wɑtʃ 〕*v.* 觀賞

People in the city can *watch* birds in the mountains.

wear 〔 wɛr 〕 *v.* 穿；戴

Have you noticed the new glasses Kevin is *wearing* today?

* notice 〔'notɪs 〕 *v.* 注意到
  glasses 〔'glæsɪz 〕 *n. pl.* 眼鏡

【典型考題】

The lady _____ a diamond ring on her finger.

(A) wore   (B) threw
(C) reached   (D) prepared

答案：**A**

weed 〔 wid 〕 *v.* 除草

My father asked me to *weed* the garden.

* garden 〔'gɑrdn̩ 〕 *n.* 花園

welcome 〔'wɛlkəm 〕 *v.* 歡迎

Mr. and Mrs. Jones *welcomed* him warmly when he return from his trip.

* warmly 〔'wɔrmlɪ 〕 *adv.* 親切地

- [ ] tow   _____
- [ ] try   _____
- [ ] wash   _____
- [ ] sour   _____
- [ ] take   _____

- [ ] tell   _____
- [ ] use   _____
- [ ] wear   _____
- [ ] touch   _____
- [ ] solve   _____

- [ ] speak   _____
- [ ] treat   _____
- [ ] vacuum   _____
- [ ] weed   _____
- [ ] waste   _____

Check List

1. 鋪　　　　s ___spread___ d
2. 歡　迎　　w _____ e
3. 觀　賞　　w _____ h
4. 自　願　　v _____ r
5. 請　客　　t _____ t

6. 使驚訝　　s _____ e
7. 抽　煙　　s _____ e
8. 教　　　　t _____ h
9. 碰　觸　　t _____ h
10. 旅　行　　t _____ l

11. 浪　費　　w _____ e
12. 說　　　　s _____ k
13. 嚐起來　　t _____ e
14. 帶　　　　t _____ e
15. 解　決　　s _____ e

wonder 〔'wʌndə 〕 *v.* 想知道

I *wonder* if the food in that famous restaurant is really that delicious.

【典型考題】

Sue is a cute girl. I _____ if she has a boyfriend.

(A) want (B) guess
(C) wonder (D) know

答案：**C**

形容詞

active ﹝'æktɪv﹞ *adj.* 活躍的；積極的

Patty is an *active* girl who
likes sports.

```
act  + ive
 |      |
活動  + adj.
```

【典型考題】

The old man always took a(n) _____
part in the movements.

(A) active   (B) alive
(C) actively   (D) activity

答案：**A**

afraid ﹝ə'fred﹞ *adj.* 害怕的

I am very *afraid* of dogs.

【典型考題】

Students are _____ of speaking English
to foreigners.

(A) afraid   (B) able
(C) legal   (D) happy

答案：**A**

allergic 〔 ə'lɝdʒɪk 〕 *adj.* 過敏的

Ann loves cats but she can't keep one as a pet, for she is *allergic* to the fur.

* pet 〔 pɛt 〕 *n.* 寵物   fur 〔 fɝ 〕 *n.* 皮毛

alone 〔 ə'lon 〕 *adj.* 單獨的

She watches TV when she is *alone*.

angry 〔'æŋgrɪ 〕 *adj.* 生氣的

Our teacher gets *angry* easily. When he is *angry*, he looks angrily at everyone.

【典型考題】

I was _____ at the boys for being late.

(A) angry   (B) happy

(C) glad   (D) calm

答案：**A**

another 〔 əˈnʌðɚ 〕 *adj.* 另一個

He became quite *another* man.

* quite 〔 kwaɪt 〕 *adv.* 相當地

asleep 〔 əˈslip 〕 *adj.* 睡著的

Kelly was so tired that she couldn't help falling *asleep* in class.

* ***help* + *V-ing*** 忍不住

```
a  + sleep
|      |
in + 睡覺
```

best-selling 〔ˈbɛstˈsɛlɪŋ 〕 *adj.* 暢銷的

The Harry Potter books are among the *best-selling* books.

black 〔 blæk 〕 *adj.* 黑色的

I prefer to write with *black* ink.

* ink 〔 ɪŋk 〕 *n.* 墨水

bored 〔 bord 〕 *adj.* （人）覺得無聊的

As a student, I feel *bored* sitting in the same classroom almost eight hours a day.

【典型考題】

I do feel _____ in the classes I don't like.
(A) boring   (B) bored
(C) interested   (D) interesting

答案：**B**

boring 〔'borɪŋ 〕 *adj.* 無聊的

It is so *boring* a story that I don't want to listen to it.

brown 〔 braʊn 〕 *adj.* （皮膚）曬黑的

Carol is very *brown* after her holiday in Australia. The sun there is very strong.

* Australia 〔ɔ'streljə 〕 *n.* 澳洲
    sun 〔 sʌn 〕 *n.* 陽光

busy ('bɪzɪ) *adj.* 忙碌的；(電話) 忙線的

I couldn't talk to Susan on the phone because the line was *busy*.

【典型考題】

He keeps himself _____ to avoid thinking about his girlfriend's death.

(A) quiet   (B) stupid

(C) busy   (D) upset

答案：**C**

careful ('kɛrfəl) *adj.* 小心的

Batters must be more *careful* because they may miss the ball easily.

* batter ('bætɚ) *n.* 打擊手
   miss (mɪs) *v.* 沒打中

careless ('kɛrlɪs) *adj.* 粗心的

He is a *careless* driver.

comfortable〔'kʌmfətəbḷ 〕 *adj.* 舒適的

The MRT is a *comfortable* way to
travel on holidays.

comfort + able
| |
舒適 + *adj.*

【典型考題】

A _____ sofa makes it easy to fall asleep.

(A) hard   (B) tough

(C) hot   (D) comfortable

答案：**D**

convenient〔kən'vinjənt 〕 *adj.* 方便的

Come and see me whenever it is
convenient for you. I'll be home all day
tomorrow.

【典型考題】

To take the MRT in Taipei is really
_____ for people without cars.

(A) soft   (B) hard

(C) ready   (D) convenient

答案：**D**

crowded 〔'kraʊdɪd 〕*adj.* 擁擠的

The MRT station was very *crowded*.

【典型考題】

In the morning, the bus is always _____

with a lot of people.

(A) full   (B) rich

(C) crowded   (D) poor

答案：**C**

daily 〔'delɪ 〕*adj.* 每天的

Reading newspapers is my *daily* work.

dangerous 〔'dendʒərəs 〕*adj.* 危險的

It is *dangerous* to go out on a typhoon day.

The sky is dark and the wind is strong.

```
danger + ous
   |        |
 危險   +  adj.
```

- [ ] careful _____
- [ ] afraid _____
- [ ] wonder _____
- [ ] comfortable _____
- [ ] careless _____

- [ ] alone _____
- [ ] dangerous _____
- [ ] allergic _____
- [ ] busy _____
- [ ] asleep _____

- [ ] boring _____
- [ ] daily _____
- [ ] angry _____
- [ ] another _____
- [ ] crowded _____

Check List

1. 想知道   w ___*wonder*___ r

2. 害怕的   a _____ d

3. 小心的   c _____ l

4. 舒適的   c _____ e

5. 過敏的   a _____ c

6. 危險的   d _____ s

7. 單獨的   a _____ e

8. 忙碌的   b _____ y

9. 睡著的   a _____ p

10. 擁擠的   c _____ d

11. 無聊的   b _____ g

12. 生氣的   a _____ y

13. 粗心的   c _____ s

14. 每天的   d_____ y

15. 另一個   a _____ r

dark 〔 dɑrk 〕 *adj.* 黑暗的

It's too *dark* in here, and I need a flashlight to help me find my way out.

delicious 〔 dɪ'lɪʃəs 〕 *adj.* 美味的

The dishes they serve in that restaurant are very *delicious*.

* serve 〔 sɜv 〕 *v.* 供應

different 〔'dɪfərənt 〕 *adj.* 不同的

The weather in Taipei is *different* from that in Tokyo.

* weather 〔'wɛðɚ 〕 *n.* 天氣

differ + ent
| |
不同 + *adj.*

difficult 〔'dɪfə‚kʌlt 〕 *adj.* 困難的

The question is so *difficult* that I can't answer it right away.

* *right away* 立刻

【典型考題】

Never give up anything _____. Maybe it's the key to success.

(A) tasty   (B) illegal

(C) difficult   (D) happy

答案：**C**

dizzy 〔'dɪzɪ 〕 *adj.* 暈眩的

When I got up from the chair, I felt *dizzy*.

* *get up* 起身

easy 〔'izɪ 〕 *adj.* 容易的

It is *easy* to keep in touch with our friends by telephone.

* *keep in touch with* 和～保持聯絡

elementary (ˌɛləˈmɛntərɪ) *adj.* 初級的

My younger brother is seven years old, so he is old enough to go to *elementary* school.

* *elementary school* 小學

embarrassed (ɪmˈbærəst) *adj.* 尷尬的

Your parents were *embarrassed* by what you did. You should apologize.

```
embarrass   +   ed
    |            |
  使尷尬       +  adj.
```

【典型考題】

Study harder, or you'll be _____ about your poor grades all the time.

(A) embarrassed　　(B) embarrassing

(C) satisfied　　(D) satisfying

答案：**A**

embarrassing 〔 ɪmˈbærəsɪŋ 〕 *adj.*
令人尷尬的

I feel falling down on the road is so
embarrassing.

```
embarrass + ing
   |          |
  使尷尬    + adj.
```

enough 〔 əˈnʌf 〕 *adj.* 足夠的

We want to buy the new color TV, but we
don't have *enough* money.

* *color TV* 彩色電視

exciting 〔 ɪkˈsaɪtɪŋ 〕 *adj.* 刺激的

It was an *exciting* game! Our class won
56-55.

famous 〔ˈfeməs 〕 *adj.* 有名的

France is *famous* for its fine food and wine.

* fine 〔 faɪn 〕 *adj.* 美好的
  wine 〔 waɪn 〕 *n.* 葡萄酒

【典型考題】

Li Po is _____ as a poet in Chinese history.

(A) private   (B) famous

(C) smart   (D) silly

答案：**B**

fashionable 〔ˊfæʃənəbl̩〕 adj. 時髦的

Your cell phone is the newest kind, isn't it? It is really *fashionable*.

fashion + able
　｜　　　｜
流行 + adj.

【典型考題】

The _____ man really caught all of the girls' eyes.

(A) plain   (B) kind

(C) wide   (D) fashionable

答案：**D**

favorite 〔'fevərɪt 〕 *adj.* 最喜愛的

Milk chocolate is my *favorite* kind of candy. I love it so much that I cannot live without it.

* *cannot live without* 不能沒有

【典型考題】

My ＿＿＿＿＿ singer is A-mei.

(A) favorite   (B) popular

(C) sick   (D) heavy

答案：**A**

fond 〔 fɑnd 〕 *adj.* 喜歡的

Tom is *fond* of playing baseball.

【典型考題】

I'm very＿＿＿＿＿ of fishing on holidays.

(A) funny   (B) fun

(C) fond   (D) foreign

答案：**C**

foreign ('fɔrɪn) *adj.* 外國的

English is studied by us as a *foreign* language.

【典型考題】

Lisa is excited about studying in a(n) _____ country.

(A) abroad (B) funny

(C) outer (D) foreign

答案：**D**

formal ('fɔrml) *adj.* 正式的

Jean came to Joe's party in *formal* dress.

fresh (frɛʃ) *adj.* 新鮮的

I like to live in the country because the air there is very *fresh*.

friendly 〔'frɛndlɪ〕*adj.* 友善的

He is very *friendly* to me.

【典型考題】

People in the country are usually more
_____ than people in the city.

(A) easy (B) living
(C) dead (D) friendly

答案：**D**

frightened 〔'fraɪtṇd〕*adj.* 害怕的

Meg was too *frightened* to be able to sleep
because she heard someone screaming.

* scream〔skrim〕*v.* 尖叫

【典型考題】

She was _____ that there might be a
ghost in the dark.

(A) fear (B) bored
(C) frightened (D) exciting

答案：**C**

🐛 自 我 測 驗

- ☐ embarrassed _____
- ☐ famous _____
- ☐ fashionable _____
- ☐ dizzy _____
- ☐ enough _____

- ☐ formal _____
- ☐ fond _____
- ☐ foreign _____
- ☐ frightened _____
- ☐ exciting _____

- ☐ delicious _____
- ☐ friendly _____
- ☐ difficult _____
- ☐ dark _____
- ☐ elementary _____

1. 有名的　　f _____famous_____ s

2. 暈眩的　　d _____ y

3. 足夠的　　e _____ h

4. 美味的　　d _____ s

5. 時髦的　　f _____ e

6. 尷尬的　　e _____ d

7. 外國的　　f _____ n

8. 困難的　　d _____ t

9. 友善的　　f _____ y

10. 刺激的　　e _____ g

11. 黑暗的　　d _____ k

12. 害怕的　　f _____ d

13. 正式的　　f _____ l

14. 喜歡的　　f _____ d

15. 初級的　　e _____ y

full〔fʊl〕*adj.* 充滿的;客滿的

The theater was *full*.

gentle〔'dʒɛntḷ〕*adj.* 溫和的

Mr. Peterson is the most *gentle* man I've ever known. He is kind to all of us.

good〔gʊd〕*adj.* 好的;有益的

Exercise is *good* for health.

greasy〔'grizɪ〕*adj.* 油膩的

The doctor suggested that the old not eat too much *greasy* food.

* suggest〔sə'dʒɛst〕*v.* 建議

   the old 老人(= *old people*)

> easy *adj.* 容易的
> greasy *adj.* 油膩的

great〔gret〕*adj.* 偉大的

The telephone is a *great* invention.

With it, we can stay in touch with our friends.

* invention〔ɪn'vɛnʃən〕*n.* 發明

  stay in touch 和～保持聯絡

healthy〔'hɛlθɪ〕*adj.* 健康的

Swimming is one of the *healthiest* forms of exercise.

* form〔fɔrm〕*n.* 形式

health + y
健康 + *adj.*

【典型考題】

Eating the right food and getting enough exercise will make you _____.

(A) worse (B) wealthy
(C) healthy (D) true

答案：**C**

heavy 〔ˈhɛvɪ〕 *adj.* 重的

The doctor says that I'm too *heavy* and I should lose weight as soon as possible.

* *lose weight* 減輕體重

【典型考題】

The luggage is too _____ for me to lift.

(A) heavy   (B) lazy

(C) rich   (D) easy

答案:**A**

hungry 〔ˈhʌŋgrɪ〕 *adj.* 飢餓的

The taxi driver was *hungry*, so he stopped at the McDonald's to get something to eat.

【典型考題】

Nothing can stop a(n) _____ man from finding food.

(A) angry   (B) hungry

(C) good   (D) busy

答案:**B**

ideal 〔 aɪˈdiəl 〕 *adj.* 理想的

It is hard for her to find an *ideal* mate, who must be rich and handsome.

* mate 〔 met 〕 *n.* 伴侶

illegal 〔 ɪˈligḷ 〕 *adj.* 非法的

It's *illegal* to store a lot of rice wine.

* store 〔 stor 〕 *v.* 儲存；囤積
rice wine 米酒

```
il  + legal
|      |
not + 合法的
```

【典型考題】

Selling drugs, guns or alcohol to children is _____.

(A) legal   (B) ideal
(C) important   (D) illegal

答案：**D**

important 〔 ɪmˈpɔrtṇt 〕 *adj.* 重要的

Enough sleep and good food are *important* to health.

impossible 〔 ɪm'pɑsəbḷ 〕 *adj.* 不可能的

It is *impossible* for any living thing in the world to live without air or water.

```
im  +  possible
 |         |
not  +  可能的
```

impressed 〔 ɪm'prɛst 〕 *adj.* 印象深刻的

After a visit to the Palace Museum, we were very *impressed* with the art treasures of our country.

* ***the Palace Museum*** 故宮博物院

treasure 〔'trɛʒɚ 〕 *n.* 寶物

```
impress  + ed
   |         |
使印象深刻 + adj.
```

【典型考題】

Everyone is so _____ with her good voice.

(A) impossible   (B) important

(C) impressed   (D) impossible

答案：**C**

interesting (ˈɪntrɪstɪŋ) *adj.* 有趣的

The book was so *interesting* that the boy found it hard to put it down.

【典型考題】

It's _____ to study people's expressions.
(A) interesting   (B) nervous
(C) interested   (D) embarrassed

答案：**A**

junior (ˈdʒunjɚ) *adj.* 年少的

After I graduate from *junior* high school, I want to go to Paris and study art.

lucky (ˈlʌkɪ) *adj.* 幸運的

In Taiwan, adults usually give their children *lucky* money on Chinese New Year's Eve.

* adult (əˈdʌlt) *n.* 成人
  lucky money 壓歲錢

```
luck  +  y
 |       |
運氣  + adj.
```

【典型考題】

He was _____ to escape being killed in that accident.

(A) unlucky   (B) lucky

(C) sorry   (D) noisy

答案：**B**

magic 〔'mædʒɪk 〕*adj.* 有魔力的   *n.* 魔術

The main character in the Harry Potter books is a boy with *magic* power.

medium 〔'midɪəm 〕*adj.* 五分熟的

"How would you like your steak?"

"I'd like it *medium*."

* steak 〔 stek 〕*n.* 牛排

messy 〔'mɛsɪ 〕*adj.* 亂七八糟的

My brother's room is always *messier* than mine.

middle （'mɪdl̩ ）*adj.* 中間的

The word in the *middle* of the sentence
"I like you." is "like."

musical （'mjuzɪkl̩ ）*adj.* 喜愛音樂的

Her family are all *musical*.

natural （'nætʃərəl ）*adj.* 自然的

He has lived in Japan for ten years,
so it is *natural* that he speaks Japanese
so well.

* Japan （ dʒə'pæn ）*n.* 日本
Japanese （ˌdʒəpə'niz ）*n.* 日語

natur	+	al
自然	+	*adj.*

nervous （'nɝvəs ）*adj.* 緊張的

Sue is a *nervous* woman.

自 我 測 驗

- [ ] great   _____
- [ ] messy   _____
- [ ] middle   _____
- [ ] gentle   _____
- [ ] junior   _____

- [ ] greasy   _____
- [ ] magic   _____
- [ ] ideal   _____
- [ ] natural   _____
- [ ] nervous   _____

- [ ] healthy   _____
- [ ] illegal   _____
- [ ] impressed   _____
- [ ] heavy   _____
- [ ] hungry   _____

1. 中間的   m ___*middle*___ e
2. 溫和的   g _____ e
3. 年少的   j _____ r
4. 油膩的   g _____ y
5. 有魔力的   m _____ c

6. 理想的   i _____ l
7. 自然的   n _____ l
8. 非法的   i _____ l
9. 緊張的   n _____ s
10. 健康的   h _____ y

11. 偉大的   g _____ t
12. 亂七八糟的   m _____ y
13. 印象深刻的   i _____ d
14. 重　的   h _____ y
15. 飢餓的   h _____ y

nosy 〔'nozɪ 〕 *adj.* 愛管閒事的

We don't like *nosy* people at all.

* **not…at all** 一點也不

past 〔 pæst 〕 *adj.* 過去的

Let me tell you about my *past* life.

polite 〔 pə'laɪt 〕 *adj.* 有禮貌的

When you ask for help, remember to be *polite*.

* remember 〔 rɪ'mɛmbɚ 〕 *v.* 記得

【典型考題】

It was _____ of her to offer the elderly man her seat.

(A) polite   (B) middle

(C) terrible   (D) healthy

答案：**A**

popular 〔'pɑpjələ 〕 *adj.* 受歡迎的

May Day has become the most *popular* band in Taiwan.

* band 〔 bænd 〕 *n.* 樂團

【典型考題】

The novelist is _____ with young people.
(A) popular   (B) filled
(C) strong   (D) thin

答案：**A**

possible 〔'pɑsəbḷ 〕 *adj.* 可能的

It was *possible* that it would rain later, so George took an umbrella with him to school.

proud 〔 praʊd 〕 *adj.* 驕傲的；光榮的

Allen is the best student in his class. His parents are *proud* of him.

* *be proud of* 以～為榮

quiet (ˈkwaɪət) *adj.* 安靜的

My mother asked me to keep *quiet* so that I wouldn't wake up my baby sister.

* *wake up* 叫醒

【典型考題】

"Be _____," the teacher said to calm down the excited pupil.

(A) diligent   (B) quiet
(C) hungry   (D) smart

答案：**B**

ready (ˈrɛdɪ) *adj.* 準備好的

Are you *ready* to go now? We don't have much time.

round (raʊnd) *adj.* 圓的；環繞的

"I want to buy a ticket to Boston."

"One-way or *round*-trip?"

* one-way (ˈwʌn,we) *adj.* 單程的
round-trip (ˈraʊnd,trɪp) *adj.* 來回的

serious 〔ˈsɪrɪəs〕*adj.* 認眞的；嚴肅的

Tom studies hard all the time; he is always *serious* about his tests and homework.

【典型考題】

Ms. Brown is the most _____ teacher in our school.

(A) actual   (B) good

(C) serious   (D) possible

答案：**C**

sharp 〔ʃɑrp〕*adj.* 尖銳的

It's safe to hug koalas, for they don't have *sharp* claws.

* hug 〔hʌg〕*v.* 抱
  koala 〔kəˈɑlə〕*n.* 無尾熊
  claw 〔klɔ〕*n.* 爪

shy 〔 ʃaɪ 〕 *adj.* 害羞的

She is so *shy* that her face turns red when she meets a stranger.

* turn 〔 tɜn 〕 *v.* 變成

sick 〔 sɪk 〕 *adj.* 生病的

I have a headache. I must be *sick*.

* headache 〔'hɛd,ek 〕 *n.* 頭痛

special 〔'spɛʃəl 〕 *adj.* 特別的

My older sister has a *special* talent for singing.

【典型考題】

It's a _____ case that has rarely happened.

(A) special   (B) classical

(C) narrow   (D) minor

答案：**A**

strict ﹝ strɪkt ﹞ *adj.* 嚴格的

Don't be so *strict* with him. After all,

he is just a kid.

* *after all* 畢竟   kid ﹝ kɪd ﹞ *n.* 小孩

【典型考題】

Although Monica is very ＿＿＿＿＿＿ with her

students, they like her very much.

(A) sleepy   (B) risky

(C) strict   (D) pleased

答案：**C**

strong ﹝ strɔŋ ﹞ *adj.* 濃的

A : How do you like your coffee?

B : I like it *strong*, with no sugar or cream.

* cream ﹝ krim ﹞ *n.* 奶精

stupid ﹝ˈstjupɪd﹞ *adj.* 笨的；愚蠢的

The little boy knows a lot of things.

He is not *stupid*.

sure 〔ʃʊr〕 *adj.* 確定的

Make *sure* that the doors and windows are locked before you go out.

* locked〔lɑkt〕*adj.* 上鎖的

【典型考題】

The general was _____ that he could defeat the enemy.

(A) afraid　　　　　(B) primary
(C) sure　　　　　(D) possible

答案：**C**

talented 〔'tæləntɪd〕*adj.* 有才華的

She has a good voice. She is a *talented* singer.

* voice〔vɔɪs〕*n.* 聲音；嗓子

tasty 〔'testɪ〕*adj.* 好吃的

Fast food, like hamburgers, fries, and pizza, is *tasty* but not good for children.

* *fast food* 速食　　fries〔fraɪz〕*n. pl.* 薯條

tempting ﹝'tɛmptɪŋ﹞ *adj.* 誘人的

The chocolate cake looks so *tempting*.

Why not have it right now?

```
tempt + ing
  |      |
引誘  + adj.
```

* have﹝hæv﹞*v.* 吃

right now 現在

thick﹝θɪk﹞*adj.* 厚的

I have never read such a *thick* book.

thin﹝θɪn﹞*adj.* 瘦的；薄的

She was very *thin* when she was in
junior high school.

【典型考題】

The opposite of the word "thick" is

＿＿＿＿＿.

(A) light　　　　(B) heavy

(C) thin　　　　(D) skinny

答案：**C**

- ☐ polite   _____
- ☐ tempting   _____
- ☐ quiet   _____
- ☐ nosy   _____
- ☐ serious   _____

- ☐ strict   _____
- ☐ stupid   _____
- ☐ special   _____
- ☐ sharp   _____
- ☐ proud   _____

- ☐ sure   _____
- ☐ shy   _____
- ☐ possible   _____
- ☐ tasty   _____
- ☐ popular   _____

Check List

1. 安靜的   q _____quiet_____ t

2. 愛管閒事的   n _____ y

3. 認真的   s _____ s

4. 嚴格的   s _____ t

5. 尖銳的   s _____ p

6. 有禮貌的   p _____ e

7. 誘人的   t _____ g

8. 驕傲的   p _____ d

9. 確定的   s _____ e

10. 害羞的   s _____ y

11. 笨　的   s _____ d

12. 特別的   s _____ l

13. 可能的   p _____ e

14. 好吃的   t _____ y

15. 受歡迎的   p _____ r

thirsty ('θɝstɪ) *adj.* 口渴的

The taxi driver was *thirsty*, so he stopped at Family Mart to get a Coke.

* Coke (kok) *n.* 可口可樂
(= *Coca-Cola*)

thirst + y
口渴　+ *adj.*

tight (taɪt) *adj.* 緊的

These pants are too *tight*. Please give me a larger size.

* pants (pænts) *n. pl.* 長褲 (= *trousers*)

tired (taɪrd) *adj.* 疲倦的

Most people always feel *tired* after school or work.

tir　+ ed
使疲倦 + *adj.*

tiring ('taɪrɪŋ) *adj.* 令人疲倦的；累人的

We went mountain climbing today.
After a *tiring* day, we all wanted to go
to bed early.

* *go mountain climbing* 去爬山

true (tru) *adj.* 真的

Is it *true* that you're going to be married
to Tom?

* *be married to* 和～結婚

twin (twɪn) *adj.* 雙胞胎的

Jack and Mark are *twin* brothers. No
wonder they are so much like.

* *no wonder* 難怪
  like (laɪk) *adj.* 相像的

unable (ʌn'ebl̩) *adj.* 不能的

He seems *unable* to swim.

underground 〔'ʌndɚ'graʊnd 〕 *adj.*
地下的

The subway is not always *underground*
in Tokyo.

under	+	ground
在～之下	+	地面

unhappy 〔 ʌn'hæpɪ 〕 *adj.* 不高興的

Tom's bad grades made his parents
unhappy.

* grade 〔 gred 〕 *n.* 成績

un	+	happy
not	+	快樂的

unusual 〔 ʌn'juʒʊəl 〕 *adj.* 不尋常的

It is *unusual* for Peter to be late.
He always comes on time.

* *on time* 準時

un	+	usual
not	+	尋常的

useful 〔'jusfəl 〕 *adj.* 有用的

Computers are *useful* machines but they can't solve all our problems.

use	+ ful
用	+ *adj.*

* machine 〔 məˈʃin 〕 *n.* 機器
  solve 〔 sɑlv 〕 *v.* 解決

【典型考題】

The computer is _____ in doing our reports.

(A) inconvenient   (B) horrible

(C) useful   (D) heavy

答案：**C**

volunteer 〔ˌvɑlənˈtɪr 〕 *adj.* 自願的

My mother decided to go to the hospital and do some *volunteer* work.

weak 〔 wik 〕 *adj.* 虛弱的

She is still *weak* after her long illness.

* illness 〔'ɪlnɪs 〕 *n.* 疾病

weekly ﹝'wiklɪ﹞ *adj.* 每週的

I got a *weekly* wage of $ 5000.

* wage ﹝wedʒ﹞ *n.* 工資

welcome ﹝'wɛlkəm﹞ *adj.* 受歡迎的

As a friend of mine, you are *welcome* in my home.

white ﹝hwaɪt﹞ *adj.* 白色的

The old man had *white* hair.

wise ﹝waɪz﹞ *adj.* 聰明的

It is *wise* of you to keep away from him.

* *away from* 遠離

wonderful ﹝'wʌndəfəl﹞ *adj.* 美好的

How *wonderful* today is!

young ﹝jʌŋ﹞ *adj.* 年輕的

Everyone, *young* or old, loves his music.

actively 〔'æktɪvlɪ 〕 *adv.* 主動地

Students should ask questions *actively*, and then the teachers can help them.

【典型考題】

Tom does his homework _____.

(A) actually   (B) almost

(C) actively   (D) hardly

答案：**C**

all 〔 ɔl 〕 *adv.* 全都

Don't give up. We will *all* stand by your side.

* *give up* 放棄   *stand by one's side* 支持某人

almost 〔 ɔl'most 〕 *adv.* 幾乎

We are very happy that it is *almost* time for summer vacation.

【典型考題】

The fire destroyed _____ all the forest.

(A) totally   (B) lovely

(C) almost   (D) probably

答案：**C**

alone 〔 ə'lon 〕 *adv.* 單獨地

She lives *alone* in a big apartment.

* apartment 〔 ə'pɑrtmənt 〕 *n.* 公寓

【典型考題】

Please leave me _____ at this moment.

(A) alone   (B) politely

(C) beautifully   (D) easily

答案：**A**

already 〔 ɔl'rɛdɪ 〕 *adv.* 已經

I have *already* finished my homework.

also (ˈɔlso) *adv.* 也

Are you *also* a student?

always (ˈɔlwez) *adv.* 總是

It is unusual for Mary to be late, because she *always* comes to work on time.

【典型考題】

Why are you _____ changing your mind?

(A) seldom　　　　(B) always
(C) heavily　　　　(D) hard

答案：**B**

anymore (ˈɛnɪmor) *adv.* 再也不

I won't believe you *anymore*.

beautifully (ˈbjutəfəlɪ) *adv.* 美麗地

When Christmas is coming, all department stores are *beautifully* decorated.

自我測驗

- [ ] anymore   _____
- [ ] underground   _____
- [ ] all   _____
- [ ] thirty   _____
- [ ] volunteer   _____

- [ ] already   _____
- [ ] welcome   _____
- [ ] tight   _____
- [ ] almost   _____
- [ ] tired   _____

- [ ] always   _____
- [ ] wonderful   _____
- [ ] unhappy   _____
- [ ] unusual   _____
- [ ] unable   _____

Check List

1. 緊 的   t _____*tight*_____ t
2. 幾 乎   a _____ t
3. 疲倦的   t _____ d
4. 總 是   a _____ s
5. 自願的   v _____ r

6. 已 經   a _____ y
7. 受歡迎的   w _____ e
8. 再也不   a _____ e
9. 口渴的   t _____ y
10. 美好的   w _____ l

11. 不高興的   u _____ y
12. 地下的   u _____ d
13. 全 都   a _____ l
14. 不尋常的   u _____ l
15. 不能的   u _____ e

both 〔 boθ 〕*adv.* 既…又~

Sara is *both* beautiful and smart.

* *both* **A** *and* **B** 既 A 且 B

【典型考題】

The book is _____ funny and instructive.

(A) born (B) brother

(C) borrow (D) both

答案：**D**

busily 〔'bɪzɪlɪ 〕*adv.* 忙碌地

Everyone in the office is working *busily*.

carefully 〔'kɛrfəlɪ 〕*adv.* 小心地

A careful person does things *carefully*.

【典型考題】

Cross the street more _____ or you may be hurt.

(A) carefully (B) suddenly

(C) casually (D) usually

答案：**A**

clearly 〔'klɪrlɪ 〕 *adv.* 清楚地

I think I need a new pair of glasses, because I can't see the words on the blackboard *clearly*.

* blackboard 〔'blæk,bord 〕 *n.* 黑板

【典型考題】

It is so noisy here. Please say it again more
_____.

(A) carefully   (B) specially
(C) usefully   (D) clearly

答案：**D**

comfortably 〔'kʌmfə·təblɪ 〕 *adv.* 舒服地

He settled himself *comfortably* in a chair.

* settle 〔'sɛtl̩ 〕 *v.* 安置

dangerously 〔'dendʒərəslɪ 〕 *adv.* 危險地

I'm sorry to hear that Mark is *dangerously* ill in the hospital.

downstairs ﹝'daʊn'stɛrz ﹞ *adv.* 在樓下

He left his glasses *downstairs*.

early ﹝'ɝlɪ ﹞ *adv.* 早地

I get up *early* every morning.

easily ﹝'izɪlɪ ﹞ *adv.* 容易地

In spring the weather changes a lot so people catch a cold *easily*.

* *catch a cold* 感冒

```
easi  + ly
 |       |
容易的 + adv.
```

【典型考題】

The engine of a BMW starts _____ even in cold weather .

(A) easily   (B) lonely

(C) likely   (D) perhaps

答案：**A**

especially ﹝ ə'spɛʃəlɪ ﹞ *adv.* 特別地

I *especially* like to eat Chinese food.

even〔'ivən〕adv. 即使

This is an easy question. *Even* a child can answer it.

fast〔fæst〕adv. 快速地

A：Did you catch what Mr. Wang said?

B：No. He spoke too *fast*.

* catch〔kætʃ〕v. 聽清楚

finally〔'faɪnḷɪ〕adv. 最後

He *finally* confessed his crime.

* confess〔kən'fɛs〕v. 承認
  crime〔kraɪm〕n. 罪

【典型考題】

It was a difficult assignment, but we have
＿＿＿＿＿＿ finished it.

(A) possibly   (B) finally

(C) hardly   (D) forever

答案：**B**

first 〔 fɜst 〕 *adv.* 第一；首先

Do you know who comes to school *first* every morning?

forever 〔 fə'ɛvə 〕 *adv.* 永遠；始終

Please tell me you will love me *forever*.

【典型考題】

Why are you ＿＿＿＿＿ making such mistakes?

(A) ever   (B) all the times

(C) forever   (D) all the same

答案：**C**

gently 〔 'dʒɛntḷɪ 〕 *adv.* 溫和地

My mom always talks to us *gently*.

【典型考題】

She spoke ＿＿＿＿＿ to the frightened child.

(A) gratefully   (B) well

(C) generally   (D) gently

答案：**D**

hard〔hɑrd〕*adv.* 努力地

Work *hard*, and you will succeed.

* succeed〔sək'sid〕*v.* 成功

【典型考題】

She works very _____.

(A) hard   (B) head

(C) hand   (D) hip

答案：**A**

heavily〔'hɛvɪlɪ〕*adv.* 大量地

The dark clouds gathered quickly and suddenly it began to rain *heavily*.

* gather〔'gæðɚ〕*v.* 聚集
  suddenly〔'sʌdn̩lɪ〕*adv.* 突然地

【典型考題】

Past experience will weigh _____ in the selection process.

(A) heavily   (B) finally

(C) probably   (D) easily

答案：**A**

here〔hɪr〕*adv.* 這裡

Here comes the bus.

highly〔'haɪlɪ〕*adv.* 非常地

The president is *highly* respected in his
country.

* president〔'prɛzədənt〕*n.* 總統

【典型考題】

The book was ＿＿＿＿＿＿ amusing.
(A) lonely　　　　　(B) alone
(C) highly　　　　　(D) hard
答案：**C**

how〔haʊ〕*adv.*（指方法）如何

I read every page of my English book again
and again. This is *how* I study English.

just〔dʒʌst〕*adv.* 正好；恰好

Studying English is *just* like playing
basketball. All you have to do is practice.

late ﹝ let ﹞ *adv.* 遲到

Peter's teacher scolded him for coming to school *late* every day.

later ﹝ˈletɚ﹞ *adv.* 以後

Mother will come back tomorrow and Father will be back three days *later*.

live ﹝ laɪv ﹞ *adv.* 實況地

The basketball game will be broadcast *live* tomorrow.

* broadcast ﹝ˈbrɔdˌkæst﹞ *v.* 廣播；播出

long ﹝ lɔŋ ﹞ *adv.* 長久地

May you live *long*.

loudly ﹝ˈlaʊdlɪ﹞ *adv.* 大聲地

Tom felt offended, so he closed the door *loudly*.

* offended ﹝ əˈfɛndɪd ﹞ *adj.* 生氣的

自我測驗

- ☐ loudly _____
- ☐ how _____
- ☐ fast _____
- ☐ both _____
- ☐ clearly _____

- ☐ downstairs _____
- ☐ just _____
- ☐ later _____
- ☐ early _____
- ☐ easily _____

- ☐ finally _____
- ☐ forever _____
- ☐ especially _____
- ☐ here _____
- ☐ heavily _____

Check List

1. 快速地　　 f _____*fast*_____ t
2. 既... 又~ 　 b _____ h
3. 在樓下 　　 d _____ s
4. 正　好 　　 j _____ t
5. 清楚地 　　 c _____ y

6. 以　後 　　 l _____ r
7. 早　地 　　 e _____ y
8. 最後地 　　 f _____ y
9. 永　遠 　　 f _____ r
10. 容易地 　　 e _____ y

11. 如　何 　　 h _____ w
12. 特別地 　　 s _____ y
13. 這　裡 　　 h _____ e
14. 大量地 　　 h _____ y
15. 大聲地 　　 l _____ y

luckily 〔ˈlʌkɪlɪ〕 *adv.* 幸運地

Luckily, I was chosen to take part in the speech contest.

* *take part in* 參加
  speech contest 演講比賽

【典型考題】

＿＿＿＿＿＿＿ I was at home when it began to rain.

(A) Lately   (B) Luckily

(C) Lowly   (D) Likely

答案：**B**

maybe 〔ˈmebɪ〕 *adv.* 也許

Maybe you're right.

most 〔most〕 *adv.* 最

In my opinion, my mom is the *most* beautiful woman in the world.

* *in one's opinion* 依某人之見

never 〔'nɛvɚ 〕 *adv.* 從未

I have *never* seen such a big clock before.

often 〔'ɔfən 〕 *adv.* 經常

Do you go swimming very *often* in summer?

once 〔 wʌns 〕 *adv.* 一次

Just try it *once* before you say you don't like it.

only 〔'onlɪ 〕 *adv.* 只有

There is *only* one student in the classroom.

perhaps 〔 pɚ'hæps 〕 *adv.* 或許

John didn't come to class today; *perhaps* he is sick at home.

【典型考題】

_____ she started to cry because she was really moved by your story.

(A) Simply   (B) Always

(C) Never   (D) Perhaps

答案：**D**

politely〔pə'laɪtlɪ〕*adv.* 有禮貌地

Always remember to talk to your teacher *politely*.

【典型考題】

John offered me his seat _____.

(A) politely   (B) patiently

(C) dangerously   (D) perfectly

答案：**A**

pretty〔'prɪtɪ〕*adv.* 非常地

Don't worry. We can have our dinner *pretty* soon.

quickly 〔'kwɪklɪ〕*adv.* 快速地

Please walk *quickly*, or we'll miss the train.

quite 〔kwaɪt〕*adv.* 相當地；非常

Many students think it's *quite* hard to learn English well.

really 〔'rɪəlɪ〕*adv.* 眞正地

My father is *really* good at gardening.

* gardening 〔'gardnɪŋ〕*n.* 園藝

【典型考題】

Tell me what you _____ think.

(A) politely   (B) really
(C) especially   (D) perhaps

答案：**B**

right 〔raɪt〕*adv.* 正確地

Only a good student can answer the question *right*.

safe〔 sef 〕*adv.* 安全地

We are so happy to see that you have
returned *safe* and sound.

* *safe and sound* 安然無恙地

seldom〔'sɛldəm 〕*adv.* 很少

People *seldom* go swimming outside
during the winter because it's too cold.

seriously〔'sɪrɪəslɪ 〕*adv.* 嚴重地

Mike got *seriously* hurt in the accident.

slowly〔'slolɪ 〕*adv.* 緩慢地

Mary did her homework *slowly*. So it
was late at night when she finished it.

```
slow + ly
  |     |
 慢的 + adv.
```

so 〔 so 〕 *adv.* 如此

She is *so* tender that everyone likes her.

* tender 〔'tɛndɚ 〕 *adj.* 溫柔的

sometimes 〔'sʌm,taɪmz 〕 *adv.* 有時候

Sometimes we will go abroad for a long
vacation to relax.

* *go abroad* 出國　　relax 〔 rɪ'læks 〕 *v.* 放鬆

still 〔 stɪl 〕 *adv.* 仍然

He is a problem child, but we *still* try our
best to help him.

* *try one's best* 盡力

strictly 〔'strɪktlɪ 〕 *adv.* 嚴格地

Don't treat your children so *strictly*.

then 〔 ðɛn 〕 *adv.* 然後

I went to SOGO department store first,
and *then* I went to the movies.

there 〔ðɛr〕*adv.* 那裡

Can you see the lovely girl over *there*?

* lovely 〔'lʌvlɪ〕*adj.* 可愛的
  over there 在那裡

today 〔tə'de〕*adv.* 今天

What are you going to do *today*?

tonight 〔tə'naɪt〕*adv.* 今晚

We are going to have a party *tonight*.

too 〔tu〕*adv.* 太

I am *too* short to play basketball.

* too…to~ 太…以致於不~

truly 〔'trulɪ〕*adv.* 真實地

Please speak *truly*. I want to know the truth.

* truth 〔truθ〕*n.* 事實

usually 〔'juʒʊəlɪ 〕 *adv.* 通常

What time do you *usually* get up?

* **get up** 起床

very 〔'vɛrɪ 〕 *adv.* 很

He walked across the bridge *very* carefully.

* across 〔 ə'krɔs 〕 *prep.* 橫越
  bridge 〔 brɪdʒ 〕 *n.* 橋

well 〔 wɛl 〕 *adv.* 很好地

Although he is just a junior high school
student, he speaks English very *well*.

yesterday 〔'jɛstə,de 〕 *adv.* 昨天

We went hiking in the mountains *yesterday*.

* **go hiking** 去健行

yet 〔 jɛt 〕 *adv.* 還沒

We have not heard from him *yet*.

* **hear from** sb. 收到某人的信

- [ ] quite _____
- [ ] then _____
- [ ] slowly _____
- [ ] there _____
- [ ] maybe _____

- [ ] well _____
- [ ] pretty _____
- [ ] sometimes _____
- [ ] never _____
- [ ] perhaps _____

- [ ] yet _____
- [ ] most _____
- [ ] seldom _____
- [ ] right _____
- [ ] really _____

🖉 Check List

1.	那　裡	t	_there_	e
2.	然　後	t		n
3.	正確地	r		t
4.	很好地	w		l
5.	非常地	p		y
6.	也　許	m		e
7.	有時候	s		s
8.	從　未	n		r
9.	或　許	p		s
10.	還　沒	y		t
11.	最	m		t
12.	緩慢地	s		y
13.	很　少	s		m
14.	相當地	q		e
15.	真正地	r		y

單字索引

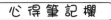

心 得 筆 記 欄

劉毅英文家教班同學獎學金排行榜

姓 名	學 校	總金額	姓 名	學 校	總金額	姓 名	學 校	總金額
謝家綺	板橋高中	40600	方predict予	北一女中	13500	吳沛璉	靜修女中	7900
王芊纍	北一女中	36850	范詠琪	中山女中	13400	俞欣妍	大直高中	7900
吳書軒	成功高中	36100	吳思慧	景美女中	13300	林妤靜	格致高中	7800
趙啓鈞	松山高中	34650	許瓊中	北一女中	13100	楊沐焓	師大附中	7750
袁好薈	武陵高中	32850	溫哲興	延平高中	12200	許瑞庭	內湖高中	7700
林怡廷	清華大學	27800	應奇穎	建國中學	12000	高維珣	麗山高中	7700
王挺之	建國中學	27200	劉楫坤	北一女中	11900	李承祐	成功高中	7700
羅之勵	大直高中	25900	廖瓦軒	武陵高中	11800	吳蜜妮	万松高中	7700
蕭允惟	景美女中	25500	盧昱瑋	格致高中	11550	林冠宏	林口高中	7600
黃筱雅	北一女中	25000	呂潘瑗	成功高中	11400	鄭懿珊	北一女中	7600
王廷鎧	建國中學	24400	陳宜蓉	中山女中	11200	林育汝	中山女中	7400
許嘉容	北 市 商	24400	蘇紀如	北一女中	11100	柯賢鴻	松山高中	7400
潘羽薇	丹鳳高中	19600	陳怡靜	北一女中	11000	張馨馨	板橋高中	7300
蘇芳萱	大同高中	19500	謝承承	大同高中	10900	陳冠廷	薇閣國小	7150
林政穎	中崙高中	18800	陳亭如	北一女中	10400	謝瑜容	中山女中	7100
郭睿豪	和平高中	18700	鄭浣心	板橋高中	10100	郭禹溱	北一女中	7000
邱瀞萱	縣格致中學	18300	何思壘	和平高中	10000	詹 羽	師大附中	6900
郭子瑄	新店高中	17500	遲定鴻	格致高中	9400	游宗憲	竹林高中	6800
柯博軒	成功高中	17500	黃靖儒	建國中學	9300	張繼元	華江高中	6600
陳瑾瑄	北一女中	16500	陳冠儒	大同高中	9200	張焘蓉	薇閣高中	6500
陳聖妮	中山女中	16400	徐子瑤	松山高中	9000	蘇瑢萱	景美女中	6400
蔡欣圃	百齡高中	16300	吳易倫	板橋高中	9000	黃崇愷	成功高中	6400
施衍廷	成功高中	15700	潘育誠	成功高中	8800	林建宏	成功高中	6300
詹皓翔	新莊高中	15500	陳庭偉	板橋高中	8800	江婉盈	中山女中	6100
廖彥綸	師大附中	15400	王千瑪	景美女中	8700	林柏翰	中正高中	6000
何俊毅	師大附中	14800	巫冠毅	板橋高中	8600	徐詩婷	松山高中	5900
陳 昕	麗山高中	14600	黃新雅	松山高中	8600	吳宇珊	景美女中	5800
簡士益	格致高中	14500	林承慶	建國中學	8600	洪珮榕	板橋高中	5700
宋才閏	成功高中	14500	謝竣宇	建國中學	8400	吳秉學	師大附中	5700
王秉立	板橋高中	14300	江 方	中山女中	8300	蔡承玘	景美女中	5600
廖崇鈞	大同高中	13800	吳念馨	永平高中	8200	王凱弘	師大附中	5600
鄭 晴	北一女中	13800	王舒亭	縣格致中學	8200	翁子惇	縣格致中學	5500
張馥雅	北一女中	13700	潘威霖	建國中學	8100			

※ 因版面有限，尚有領取高額獎學金同學，無法列出。

LE 劉毅英文教育機構

台北市許昌街17號6F（捷運M8出口對面・學善補習班）　　TEL：（02）2389-5212
台中市三民路三段125號7F（光南文具批發樓上・劉毅補習班）　TEL：（04）2221-8861

國中七年級會考模考班

●課程規劃

科　目	星　期	上課時間
數　學　科	週　六	晚上6:30~9:30
英　文　科	週　六	下午2:00~5:00
自　然　科	週　日	下午3:30~5:30
國　文　科	週　日	下午1:30~3:30

■ 背書制度：依每學期公佈指定背書之項目
　　　　　　優先背完前200名同學，可得
　　　　　　獎學金1,000元！

●獎學金辦法

科目	項目	獎學金	注意事項
數學科	段考滿分獎	1,000元	1. 憑學校段考成績，可得 　　獎學金1,000元。
英文科	段考滿分獎	1,000元	2. 限報名該單科課程，且 　　每科目限領乙次。
自然科	段考滿分獎	1,000元	3. 每學期最高可領5,000元。
國文科	段考滿分獎	1,000元	4. 依獎學金申請規定辦理。

★ 小六升國七同學，可憑市長獎申請5,000元獎學金！

劉毅英文教育機構 學費最低・效果最佳

台北本部：台北市許昌街17號6F（學善補習班）　　TEL：（02）2389-5212
台中總部：台中市三民路三段125號7F（劉毅補習班）TEL：（04）2221-8861
www.learnschool.com.tw

國中八年級會考模考班

●課程規劃 ✎

科　目	星　期	上課時間
會 考 英 文	週　六	下午2:00~5:00
數　學　科	週　日	早上10:00~12:00
自　然　科	週　日	下午1:30~3:30
國　文　科	週　日	下午3:30~5:30

■背書制度：依每學期公佈指定背書之項目
　　　　　　優先背完前200名同學，可得
　　　　　　獎學金1,000元！

●獎學金辦法 ✎

科目	項目	獎學金	注意事項
數學科	段考滿分獎	1,000元	1.憑學校段考成績，可得 　獎學金1,000元。
英文科	段考滿分獎	1,000元	2.限報名該單元課程，且 　每科目限領乙次。
自然科	段考滿分獎	1,000元	3.每學期最高可領5,000元。
國文科	段考滿分獎	1,000元	4.依獎學金申請規定辦理。

劉毅英文教育機構 學費最低．效果最佳

台北本部：台北市許昌街17號6F（學善補習班）　　TEL：(02) 2389-5212
台中總部：台中市三民路三段125號7F（劉毅補習班）　TEL：(04) 2221-8861
www.learnschool.com.tw

★ 國中會考5A保證班

　劉毅老師為慶祝劉毅英文開班42週年,特別推出「劉毅國中會考5A履約保證班」,保證同學於「國中教育會考」中達到5科A級分,符合約定內容,最後未能達標,學費全退。

■ 課程包含: 1. 寒、暑假特訓班+寒、暑假戰鬥營:上課、自習、考試、輔導,突破學習瓶頸。

2. 全科總複習+黃金猜題班:循環式主題複習,目標達到科科A級分。

3. 免費提供高中升學諮詢服務。

4. 凡「劉毅國中會考5A保證班」學生,報名「中級英檢」課程,5折優待。

5. 國中教育會考5科A級分,劉毅高一英文班同學,可領獎學金1萬元。

1.
會考成績
保證

2.
全科循環
複習

3.
最新升學
資訊

4.
英語認證
優惠

5.
會考高額
獎金

▶上課時間 ✎

	星期六	科　目	星期日	科　目
早	9:00~12:00	開放免費來班自習	8:30~10:30	週　考
			10:30~12:30	數學科
午	2:00~5:00	會考英文(含聽力)	1:30~3:30	國文科
			3:30~5:30	自然科
晚	6:3~9:30	精密研讀輔導解惑	6:30~8:30	社會科
			8:30~9:30	週　考

升高中關鍵 500 字

主　　　編/劉　毅

發　行　所/學習出版有限公司　☎ (02) 2704-5525

郵　撥　帳　號/05127272 學習出版社帳戶

登　記　證/局版台業 *2179* 號

印　刷　所/裕強彩色印刷有限公司

台 北 門 市/台北市許昌街 10 號 2 F　☎ (02) 2331-4060

台灣總經銷/紅螞蟻圖書有限公司　☎ (02) 2795-3656

本公司網址　www.learnbook.com.tw

電 子 郵 件　learnbook@learnbook.com.tw

> 售價：新台幣一百八十元正

2016 年 3 月 1 日新修訂